OCEAN SALT

BOOK 1: THE ALLAGI

A.W. MILLER

First paperback edition November 2020

Book cover design by A.W. Miller

ISBN 978-1-7361493-2-4 (paperback)

ISBN 978-1-7361493-1-7 (ebook)

www.awmiller.tesseraproductions.com

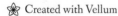 Created with Vellum

This novel as it appears here would not be possible if not for the love, support, wisdom, and Southern strength of my own beloved Earthsider, my best friend, my fellow beachbum, my noshuun...my wife Terri.

I love you forever and a day, baby.

PROLOGUE

"Your life must be forfeit or the Sisters will know our bargain comes under false pretenses," his elder brother spoke grimly, knowingly.

"They will smell the ruse," his younger brother intoned moodily.

The smell of this place reminded him of his childhood. Earth and roots mingling with damp air and salt. He took in a long, deep breath, weary already of this bickering among his brothers. He chose his words carefully.

"I have died before," he responded more coldly than he'd intended, his voice clapping back to him from the walls of this *diamesos,* the Halfway. Another memory bloomed in his mind: Their first time playing here as boys. They alone knew of this wondrous place between their world and the world for which they were responsible.

"They cannot smell their own wretched arses," the eldest of them chuckled darkly.

"I would that I had their filthy robes in my hands right now to choke—"

"Be at ease, brother. Speak not of them in this place lest

they take that from us as well." The elder brother in a squat, doodled idly with his fingers in the grit which covered the gray stone floor. To his right lay the enormous lapis lazuli disc upon which they had emblazoned their mark. The work had taken them centuries, connecting all the conduits, hiding every little....

"How am I to be at ease when *this* is happening to me?" the youngest of them screeched without meaning to, his voice not entirely under his control. He gestured frantically to the rich brown locks of his once white hair.

"Not as bad as Enyalius," he offered by way of comfort but he could see that his youngest brother took none from it. He thought of his friend, now adrift and mad and wondered if that fate would befall them all should their plans fail.

"What of the *Dunamis*, brother?" the eldest asked.

He toed the edge of the disc which rose but a centimeter above the stone floor. Beneath it lay more trouble than Pandora's Box, if their plans failed. He paced around the massive circle, remembering the hours they'd spent here in the Halfway, playing. Playing as boys will play. Would they still have played at war had they known the truth of the war to come?

"Yes, the *Dunamis*! You cannot take it with you, you know. It will never work!" the youngest of them had become, ornery as of late. Moody and ornery, worse than a woman entering her courses, he thought.

"It shall be split thrice." He spoke calmly, thinking only about his boyhood. To think of her right now would weaken his resolve. And yet she came to his heart with all the potency of a stolen kiss. He wished she were here to do just that.

"Hmm, and to whom have you tasked the role of courier? You cannot complete the Allagi without it, brother." The eldest stood and joined him in his waltz around the disc that hid a thousand roads.

"The boy," he replied.

"*Him*?" the youngest belched. "You're giving the Dunamis to the boy who flits about with a head full of—"

"Yes. He is more than you grant him worthy of, little brother. Upon my death he will retrieve his third and then—"

"Please do not tell me you've tasked your *oikonomos*...." the almost boy who was once a regal man pouted. "You did didn't you?"

"Again yes. A third to the boy, a third to Amynta and a third to my beloved."

Both of his brothers fell silent and still.

"You cannot allow her to know the truth." The eldest, always pragmatic, squeezed his shoulders drawing his face up to look directly into his eyes. "This is too dangerous already and involving her means—"

"Is it not what we are after in the end?" He spoke firmly, thinking of his eldest brother many years ago laying atop the spot where the disc now sat, reading poetry and telling of his love for a borrowed girl....

"If we fail in this then all she knows will fail, all we know will fail. Perhaps we have waited too long..." the youngest collapsed atop the disc. The Blight had come upon him unexpectedly, corrupting and reducing him to this mess of a man-child.

"We have waited too long, in that you are correct brother. Diplomacy could not stop this. Direct confrontation could not stop this. But we cannot ignore the gift of my beloved's arrival and we must seize it before the Sisters learn the truth and undo all of this." He gestured widely to encompass not only all of the Halfway, but each of them as well. Their stories which brought them here to the end.

The eldest sat beside the youngest and embraced him with one arm, pulled him close. "It is the only way to undo what curses you now."

The younger brother took a deep breath, his eyes cloudy with age but his body stuck somewhere between man and boy.

They peered up at him invitingly.

He smiled and sat beside them, thinking of times passed when they would sit together in this place and make wishes by tossing stones upward into the blackness. The silence held them for a long while.

"Are you frightened?" his eldest brother asked at last.

"Of death? No." he answered.

"Of the *Allagi*?" The younger brother whispered.

He thought a moment before replying. "Some. It has not been attempted by one such as we...not since the Elders, at least." He thought of her again, her black curls, her long fingers, her twinkling laugh. "My greatest fear is facing her in the wake of my lies."

"Aye," the eldest agreed. "Then perhaps all of our efforts will be for naught and we lose to the three hags and you'll never have to face your beloved." He laughed heartily, a booming sound that warmed the Halfway temporarily.

"I am frightened of what's next," the youngest said weepily.

The elder brothers embraced the younger and for a long moment they simply held each other.

In the quiet, he allowed himself to imagine what was next for him and his beloved. If she forgave him for lying to her for a year, duping her into believing he was something other than Poseidon? Would she remain his beloved if they survived what was to come?

He pushed the worry away and returned to the memory of him and his brothers as boys, playing their war games in a place hidden from all eyes but theirs.

ONE

"Laurie."

Paul's voice?

"Laurel Nash, awaken; the hour of my death is here."

Laurel pulled her brain from sleep like a sliver from her palm; she winced at the crisp moonlight filling the circular room. *Wherewhowhat* tumbled through her brain before she gained her bearings and remembered she was in Paul's lighthouse.

"Paul? Did you..." she could not finish her words with his mouth on her lips. She took in his kiss as she always did, with the same electric harmony she'd experienced the first time almost a year ago. "I dreamt of that boy again," she started but Paul lifted her out of bed, his strength astounding.

"Aye? It is three times now...I lament that I cannot share your dream-story, my beloved. I...this Paul...will be dead to you before dawn breaks."

Laurel's eyes had not adjusted to the moonlit dimness, but her ears had and she grabbed Paul's face, making him look into her eyes. "Don't you dare say it! You said not to worry, you told me—you promised me nothing was wrong three weeks ago! What the hell's happening? Paul!? Paul talk to me."

"Now is not the time for me to lay it all out for you, my love. I only wished to...steal one more kiss from you."

She stopped him from kissing her. "What do you mean this Paul will be dead to me?" She searched about for her chiton, suddenly apprehensive about being naked in front of him. He, however, had no qualms about his physique. The salted black hairs carpeting his chest drew her hands just as easily as his marine blue eyes pulled her toward him. No! There's something wrong, something missing and unspoken, she could feel it in her bones.

Listen to them bones, lil' fin—they're your true compass— Dad's haunting voice hadn't crept into her thoughts since she'd been with Paul. "What's wrong?" she demanded, ignoring the urgency in her dead father's voice.

"My destiny." He laughed dryly and without humor.

"What?" her voice came sharply, matching tone with that her of incessant father—*No! Not her father—her damnable conscience that happened to sound like her father*. This is happening now. "Paul, I—" she started, swallowed back her words and then started again. "Please. Tell me. I want to know what's wrong." She resisted the urge to rush out and find someone to help, fearful that doing so would rob her of their precious few remaining moments.

His chuckle darkened as he walked over to the window overlooking his island and the restless ocean. His naked body pulsed in the mercurial light now, reminding her of their lovemaking, and it struck her hard that all of this was about to end.

"I need you to listen and forget." He turned from the

window, the long black waves of his hair throwing silver shadows about the room.

"Forget? Paul, please...ugh! Where the hell is my robe?" she threw pillows and sheets about the room in search of it. "I want to know the truth. I want to know what you mean. You cannot be dying."

"I am. All of this is." He watched her the way she'd seen him watching her for the last few weeks: fondly, distracted...searching.

"You can't—no...no, everything I have is *here*! There's nothing back in Hatteras, hell I don't even have Dad's ship—if you die then—fuck! Fuck where is my robe!"

"You are every bit the Earthsider she said you were..." again he laughed his charcoal chuckle. He moved upon her and pulled his nakedness against him and she let him. She let him be as close as she possibly could and it was still not enough.

"No," she uttered softly.

He either didn't hear her or he ignored her protest. She moved to step back from him.

"My heart, my anchor, my—" he purred against her neck.

"Stop," she tried again fighting to resist his tenderness.

"I cannot," he whispered.

This time she did pull back from him, raising her hand to ward against further advances.

"There she be, my love." He held her with his gaze. A look that cut through her growing ire. He took a long, deep breath and began. "Be wary of things familiar to you, Laurie. When dawn opens her eyes upon this island, everything will change and there is nothing I can do to alter the path before us. Know this, though: I have not set you upon it without aid, or without a map. Already I can feel their grimy, decrepit fingers clawing at my Threads. I have been too long in this form."

Laurel snatched her chiton from beneath the bed, throwing it on without bothering to tie it. She put her hands to his face and made him see her. "I'm lost, Paul. I don't know what you're saying. Earthsider? Threads? What is *happening* here? I'm afraid to toss out a cliché, but you're not giving me much to work with. Another woman? You're leading a secret life—"

He laughed heartily and kissed her again.

"Stop doing that, I can't think when you kiss me like that."

He kissed her again, longer. A farewell.

"No...no...you—" she was going to say *promised* and then realized that he never had. He'd never really told her much of anything and she never really bothered to ask. *Because you knew*, her father's voice again. *You knew in your bones.*

"Something is wrong, Laurie, of that you are correct. When the morning rises you will not remember much of this moment. But with distance and time you will recover enough. I fear, though, that the Sisters will find a way between those cracks and take away all of it. Curse the lot of them for their meddling...I love you, Laurie there is nothing but truth in that."

"Paul," she knew she was crying and she hated it. She hadn't cried since leaving Hatteras—not even when Dad's ship went down. She pressed on. "Ok, what, what!? It's cancer, isn't it?" She knew it wasn't but didn't know what else to say. She wanted to shake him out of this, cut to the quick and return to the life they'd been living together for the last several months. "Listen, there are wonderful treatments available now—we can go to Athens or back to the States—"

"NO!" he thundered, silvery filaments whispering off his body.

Laurel stepped back. His six and a half foot frame withered when she did, his left hand beckoning for her to come back.

"I am sorry, my love. Sorry for keeping you." He took her face in his hands, kissed her forehead, nose, chin, and then lips as he had done the first night he'd shared his love with her. He tapped the owl's head pendant dangling between her breasts. "She will protect you after I am gone."

Laurel laid her hand atop his, pressing the pendant into her sternum. "I want _you_ to protect me from whatever it is... please talk to me! Just tell me!" she pleaded with him.

"I am forbidden; bound by the laws I cannot explain and yet I would bring down all of Olymp—" He stopped and shifted to the window so quickly she could have sworn he hadn't moved at all.

Laurel struggled to absorb the moment. None of it made sense and yet in some way she had felt it coming. Like Dad knew a storm lay miles off or a hidden shoal cowered beneath waters where no map showed its presence.

"_Anánkā d'oudè theoì mákhontai_, my love." He looked far away, sorrowful, and terribly handsome. "Not even the gods can fight necessity"

"What the hell is that supposed to mean?" She wanted to pull him close and stop all of this but her bones thrummed a dissonant chord and she knew dark waters lay ahead.

"I shall miss you Laurie. I shall miss our late night readings, a shared bottle of merlot on the beach...your stories of teaching in Cape Fear." His fingers traced her lips.

"Paul..."

Laurel's senses suddenly flared all at once. She smelled

the salt of the ocean and a dead fish in the surf; she heard gulls and their cackling poetry; she could feel the individual threads of her robe; she tasted Paul's lips upon her mouth. And then a plug was pulled and she felt nothing. Not a single sensation, not even her own breath.

The moment remained suspended and she was certain Paul spoke to her.

But she heard nothing, saw nothing, and felt *everything*.

She felt water trickling down her back, soothing and refreshing. She felt the night breeze off the ocean somehow cool and warm at the same time. She did not want the sensation to end.

When it did, the world swooped back in with a visceral punch that pushed Laurel onto the bed.

Paul moved impossibly fast to cushion her fall. He kissed her again and then darted about the room gathering up items from places Laurel didn't even know existed. Did he reach into the painting of the lilies? Had he lifted a chunk of the travertine floor? In a silvery burst he finished, dressed in his chlamys and sandals, a satchel over his shoulder. "You are the reason, you know. If not for you...none of this would be happening and all of this would be for naught. But for you, I would give them the reigns of the oceans."

"Let's go back to bed." She spoke lazily, all the words wanted to come out at the same time. "Lay beside me, please." She felt an urgency she could not identify but it faded the moment Paul moved in beside her.

"Ssshh...you are right, my beacon...you are right. *Do not allow them to keep you...do not let her touch you. Stay near the lighthouse.* I will hold you until you return to your dream."

Laurel fought the listlessness spilling over her. Something is wrong, stay awake. Fight this, she ordered her consciousness to obey even as she slipped into Paul's arms and let herself be carried into the bed. She felt him cover her, felt his body pressing against her, felt the breath of his words on her neck. *I love you,* he said and then, *I am not gone...find me Laurie...find me.*

She slept but did not dream.

TWO

It took Paul a moment to pull away from Laurel.

He had waited too long already and the waiting had nearly destroyed centuries of planning. If he could, he would tell her everything. But too many opposed he and his brothers beliefs; and though none of them were any more powerful than him, they could do things he could not.

They could hurt Laurel in ways that could not be healed or undone.

He whispered, *I love you Laurie* but did not yet leave her side. She slept unwillingly; he regretted that. He wondered if she would forgive him for tricking her. He had never loved a woman more than Laurel Nash. And he realized for the first time in a very, very long time, that he actually *felt* nervous, perhaps even fear about the future.

This made him smile because it would not have been so without her arrival nearly a year ago.

Amidst the fear, however, doubt festered and he found he could not so easily dismiss it now. Certainly a consequence of having postponed tomorrow's pomp and circumstance. He hated tradition almost as much as he hated the Fates—

The air bristled at the window, shimmering as if it were water. "I know brother," he said lightly in Greek in case Laurie should somehow awaken. He knew it was impossible, but she was an Earthsider and not at all like any woman from here.

"Now or the witches will surely intervene *again*." His brother's simmering voice did not hasten him as it should.

He found that he wanted to quit and stay here with Laurel, just watching her sleep. But doing so meant that all of what he knew, all of what he and his brothers had fought to protect...all of what Laurel cherished back home would be gone.

Forever.

He loved her too much to stay.

"Find me Laurie," he said in English. "I am not gone. Find me."

And then, Paul Okeanos died.

THREE

Laurel watched as the blind men carried Paul's body to the shallop waiting in the surf. Her fingers drifted toward the owl's head pendant, stopped and adjusted her hair instead. The braiding was far too tight and the shells had begun to dig into her scalp. Why had Amynta insisted on fixing her hair so? The woman had practically forced Laurel to stay in the lighthouse instead of being out here to say goodbye to Paul.

Her hand dropped and hovered over the owl's head again and she felt Paul's voice drift through her like a ghost.

She resisted. The words came anyway: *Something's wrong.*

Laurel turned but no one stood around her. Amynta remained in the lighthouse while Old Poppa and Ulgos tended to the outbuildings. The sisters had yet to appear.

The air blossomed with the pungent aroma of hyacinth torches burning fitfully, struggling to fill the dusk with meager light. Amynta's twin boys, Harlan and Oli, ran from stake to stake in an almost comical dance to keep the torches lit in the strong ocean breeze rolling across the beach. The toe-headed twins waved and giggled at her as they went about their task. A mischievous wind off the ocean snuck between the boys and extinguished two torches before it rippled around Laurel, stirring up sand devils before dancing off again.

She remembered the first time she stood on this beach after recovering from the sinking of her dad's ship. She had been dropped off by the old man who'd rescued her; Amynta had escorted her to the huts where she met Paul Okeanos for the first time. He had been working on repairing the thatched roof of Amynta's hut. Messy black strands of hair clung to his dirty face and blood had begun to cake around his fingertips. But Laurel had found him radiant, wonderfully unkempt and funny.

As Laurel continued to walk along the beach, she remembered many firsts with Paul. Dancing, eating Psari Plaki... kissing. She smiled to keep the tears back, the fingers of her left hand clenching the owl's head, her body longing to feel the press of Paul's body against hers again.

She crossed the sands toward the six women dressed in sheer ochre robes. Their song drifted over the sands as a single voice, glistening as did their eyes. She thought about Hatteras, and about her father's death. She revisited the voyage across the Atlantic and then, like the song of the chorus, her thoughts drifted out and away across the ocean as she continued walking away from the lighthouse.

Where am I going? She laughed a little and then felt silly because this was not a moment for laughter. Paul was dead—

I am not gone.

Laurel stopped walking.

His voice whirled through her, she was sure of it. But again, no one had approached her since the burial preparations had begun. Except for the chorus, she stood alone on the beach.

Old Poppa squinted at her out of his wrinkled eyes as he emerged from among the buildings. His broad, sun ripened chest did not puff up nor did he offer her advice on life or love. She tried to smile and failed. Old Poppa watched her for a moment, his face taut as stone, he seemed about to call out to her, but turned instead toward the huts.

It was impossible not to think of her father around Old Poppa. The two men had been carved from ocean salt, hard and pervasive and more stubborn than barnacles on a hull.

What would Nathan Nash have made of this place? Her father had talked endlessly about visiting Greece. He should have been here instead of Laurel. He had spent his entire life, during his tour in the Coast Guard and all of his retirement, planning his voyage to Greece on his beloved *Ghost*.

A strange thing occurred to her: she had lived on this island in the Mediterranean an entire year and had *never* actually visited Greece. In fact, she hadn't really had much contact with the outside world at all.

Paul always took care of everything.

She had nothing without Paul, now. This worried her. Without Paul she'd have to leave the island and try explaining to the authorities how it was she managed to stay without a passport, or identification—all of it presently submerged beneath the Mediterranean Sea.

And if she did manage to get back home to Hatteras, North Carolina...what then?

Ha! There was nothing there! She'd sold Dad's house, rented her condo out indefinitely—oh well that doesn't even begin to address the fact that she had probably been declared dead...lost at sea.

I'm lost on land, Paul. I need you. I don't want to go back.

Laurel found herself now caught within the thinning

shadow of the lighthouse. *I can't even look at it.* But she stayed in the shadow, hoping for another whisper or touch from Paul.

But Paul is dead.

The words hit like a sledgehammer to her heart but she could not feel any pain. Was it shock then? It was disbelief and anger and....

Laurel knew it was all of those things and none of them. She'd felt them before when her dad died—but that was worse. Much worse because she could have saved her father if she hadn't been such a terrible daughter.

Get back to the lighthouse, she ordered herself. Paul had told her to stay near the lighthouse. Right?

No.

Yes, he had—last night. He held her close and kissed her and he said...he said....

The memory fluttered away on the ocean breeze. "Just go back to the lighthouse," she muttered to herself. As she turned to face the lighthouse, Laurel spotted two of the three sisters.

Makaisi and Mira stood outside their hut foremost among the others; their hands gesturing elaborately in their secret sign language. They seemed distracted by something beyond Paul's funeral shallop. But the pair had always behaved peculiarly, always appearing whenever was most inconvenient. Only their older sister, Mathropos, could exceed their unorthodox behavior.

Suddenly apprehensive, Laurel scanned the beach for Mathropos. *Where's the old wretch lurking,* she wondered. Paul had frequently called her the Keeper, never offering to explain the nickname. In fact, as she thought about it, Paul always managed to explain away any strangeness upon the island.

Makaisi stopped in mid-whisper as if she'd caught some of Laurel's thoughts. Mira turned as well, her face unreadable at this distance. The pair melted back into the darkness of their hut, probably in search of Mathropos.

Something is wrong, Paul had explained last night. The *something* remained elusive, but Laurel had been feeling it for days, weeks even. She'd felt it in her bones and her bones never lied.

Lil'fin, your bones will never lie to you; they'll creak out a weather forecast, they'll hum your death knells, and sometimes they'll chime right along with a lie as it's been told to ya. It was the clearest most potent memory she'd had of her father since arriving on the island.

Laurel stopped walking and took hold of the owl's head pendant and silver light filled her thoughts.

FOUR

Old Poppa watched the Earthsider wandering back and forth along the beach.

How he wanted to go to her now...put her off the island now before the witches could sink their filthy fingers into her and wreak havoc with the girl's Threads! But he could not, dared not betray his oath. He put a hand on his son's shoulder to ease him as Laurel once again stopped her ambling walk along the beach.

"Why has she strayed from the lighthouse, father?" Ulgos stepped away from the huts but Old Poppa restrained him.

"Amynta could not keep her forever, son. She must come to awareness on her own or else she'll never escape the island or evade the witches."

Ulgos grunted.

Take up the aegis girl! He wanted to shout it but kept himself still. Soon, he knew, soon she would know.

But he would miss this blissful past, he knew. Things had been...how had Ulgos described the last year? Suspended. Yes, everything had been suspended for her...because of her. It had been a good time. A quiet time.

"Father, she holds the pendant." Ulgos started forward again and again he had to restrain his son.

"Patience, Ulgos. Let it come to her. She does not know anything more than what the old bull has allowed her to know. The discovery will not settle lightly."

Old Poppa watched as Laurel Nash changed forever.

FIVE

At first, Laurel floated inside the light. She thought she still felt the sand between her toes, and could still smell the ocean air.

A memory ricocheted out of the silver light like a warning shot:

I made this for you....

I hope it's not another palm-frond bikini....

No, but you were quite fetching in that...this is something else...

A necklace?

A pendant...my people would call this an aegis...I give it to you with all its wards and wonders.

Paul, it's exquisite...the detail of the owl's head is...oh my God! How did you—never mind—it's another one of your little magic tricks. I love it. Thank you.

Laurel wanted to move but she could not release the pendant.

She had time to take in a deep breath and then everything changed.

She had been awakened by Paul in the room at the top of

the lighthouse. The air still sizzled from their lovemaking, her body circuitry not quite reset. They had been laying front to back, his left arm encircling her chest and cupping her right breast and he was breathing deeply and evenly and it was all she ever wanted. And then there was silver light all around and she became angry and Paul soothed her and she remembered returning to sleep—but that wasn't the truth.

"I shall miss you Laurie. I shall miss our late night readings, a shared bottle of wine on the beach...your stories of teaching in Cape Fear."

She remembered his fingers tracing her lips and then they lay down...but that memory was only a bandage, a protection from Paul...

The truth overtook her.

"Laurie I wish I had the luxury of time... to explain all of it; to apologize for duping you...nothing of what I say shall make any sense to you until, I fear, it is too late. The fault is all mine, my love. I should not have brought you into this but...you have captured my heart...and it is yours to keep, I pray that will not change despite these truths I am about to speak"

None of this happened, Laurel thought, her hands squeezing the pendant so hard she was sure it would be crushed. But it did. Her bones confirmed it.

While she had been experiencing the sensation of soothing water running down her back, Paul had laid his forehead against hers and he whispered to her:

" I am Poseidon, ruler of the seas of Olympos and Earth and I am impossibly in love with you, Laurel Nash. There are rules by which I am governed, rules that make me what I am but I would change these rules for you—and to do so I must die, and return Earthside. But there are some among the gods of Olympos who believe those rules are immutable and so will

keep us apart and will do everything in their power to keep me from doing what I know in my heart is right and true.

"You must not leave this lighthouse, Laurie—do you understand me? You must not leave this lighthouse until the crest of Phoebus touches the horizon—only then will it be safe, only then can you be freed to come find me. Trust Ulgos and Old Poppa—do not walk with the sisters—are you listening?— do not walk with the sisters else they will see this dialogue and know what I have set in motion by telling you. When you awaken this body you know will be dead and I will be again in the diamesos traveling to Anaktoro where the Allagi will occur—you must reach the second lighthouse within four days' time, speak with Athena and she will guide you the rest of the way. I cannot say more, I dare not say more—already you are fighting this truth, I can feel it and the pain of your heart breaks mine, but a thousand by a thousand deaths I would endure to have your smile shine upon me just once more—this dance is at an end Laurie, find me—help me so we can dance again as one.

The truth released her and Laurel dropped the pendant.

She had no breath, her balance left her and she collapsed, sand scattering all around her.

And then she spoke what her bones had known all along:

"I'm in love with Poseidon."

SIX

Old Poppa and Ulgos approached Laurel now from behind the low buildings gathered at the base of the lighthouse. They spoke softly to one another, chiseling away at their grief, neither man familiar with such tools.

Amynta watched them through the windows as she descended the lighthouse steps. She smiled thinly, fearfully. The world was about to change and she could not be more terrified. Oli and Harlan did not understand any more than the Earthsider. But she knew. And now it had begun and it could not be stopped no matter what any of them did. Only the Earthsider could see it through.

Amynta was not convinced the girl could achieve what the gods had fought so long to regain. As she dried her tears, she watched Laurel and felt only love for the Earthsider. How many times had she almost secreted Laurel to the tip of the island to show her the truth? Her master had bound her in oath, though. Truthfully, Amynta had no regrets for only wonderful things had come of the last year. Oli and Harlan had forgotten the war that had claimed their father. Amynta had thrown herself into caring for her master and his new love.

She wished now that none of it had to end.

But Olympos could not endure the absence of its Earth-sider bond; she believed what Poseidon had told them.

She believed it with her whole self.

"I believe," she said aloud as Laurel Nash stood from the sands to face the first of her trials. Amynta continued down the stairs, silently repeating her convictions.

SEVEN

"It is wrong," Old Poppa said, dusting sand from Laurel's chiton. "They cannot do this to the old bull."

"I would choke them with their own strings if I could," Ulgos chewed down the words through clenched teeth.

Laurel watched Old Poppa. She did not feel well at all. "Is he really dead?" she tried to ask, her words jumbled and thick. *Paul is Poseidon*, she repeated in her head and then tried to speak the words. Only gibberish came out.

"Be at ease, Poet", Old Poppa soothed. He took her hand, his eyes scanning the beach in a panic.

"I think something's wrong, Old Poppa," she finally managed, though the words still didn't feel normal.

The old man whispered something to his son who moved quickly away down the beach toward the shallop holding Paul's body.

Paul or Poseidon? Laurel struggled to stay focused, feeling as if her dendrites had overloaded from the contact with the pendant.

"Their meddling has begun then," Old Poppa moved beside Laurel and spoke hastily under his breath. "Be prepared, Poet—we can deceive them but once.   Be you ready when the stones fly, aye?"

"I don't understand, Old Poppa. I think I'm supposed to be in the lighthouse."

"It is too late for that, Poet...too late for many things. The witches approach—take hold of the aegis—" and then Old Poppa was gone. Laurel blinked and he was gone. She found him walking quickly with Ulgos, both men examining the shallop.

"This must end, child." Makaisi's thickly accented voice floated to her.   Her speech always reminded Laurel of a foreign instrument played in professional hands, but still an alien sound.   The woman herself was handsome, deep-set green eyes, long elegant fingers, thick auburn hair always combed and tightly braided atop her head in a spiral. Makaisi stood nearly two inches taller than Laurel, her angular frame moved gracefully, almost measured, her words chosen in much the same manner.

Laurel moved to follow Old Poppa and Makaisi moved two times to be sure she blocked Laurel's path. The woman's face reminded Laurel of Audrey Hepburn, save for the finger-wide, one inch long scar hovering over her left eye. Laurel finally met her opalescent green eyes, the whites cracked by redness.

"What do you mean, 'this must end'?" Laurel asked bracing herself.

"Only what needs be done, daughter of Nash. It has started. Your return." Makaisi's thick voice fell out of her mouth, the words thinned by her accent, not chopped or broken but refined, well-chosen.

Laurel sifted through her memory of the last year for some clue about the true form of the sisters. Paul always deferring to them or ushering them away, sometimes making excuses to speak to them privately. For a while she thought they were bothersome, overbearing and meddlesome aunts. But now she knew: If Paul was Poseidon then these three sisters were The Fates. Her brain began dredging up fragments of Greek mythology when Makaisi dabbled her fingers in the air and Laurel's thoughts spun out of control.

Mira's laugh came from the right; the sound of cobblestones rolling in a swift-moving brook.   Laurel turned, alarmed, the two sisters flanking her.

*I have to get away from them—I don't know what they can do!   I don't know anything—*yes you do*—this is* mythology. But Laurel couldn't be sure about anything right now.   Not her memories, not her rather fragmented recollection of Greek mythology.   She certainly hadn't come to grips yet with the fact that she'd fallen in love with the god of the oceans.

Take hold of the aegis Old Poppa had admonished her. Before she could, though, Mira's hand pulled Laurel's left hand away from the pendant.

"Be at ease, Daughter of Nash—we only want to walk with you...mourn with you."   Makaisi took Laurel's right hand and patted it, her skin velvety and warm.

Mira frowned at Laurel, a grandmother made of wood. Her short fat body and mottled skin had the look and texture of a wood carving, stained and mellowed wood that has spent years under the sun, but nourished and polished by smiles and laughter. Mira's black eyes twinkled in the setting sunlight, hovering in the moist bark of her face like a pair of obsidian stones. When she spoke, the tender baritone of her voice lulled Laurel's panic. "Indeed, child, you will go and, though I am sure I risk Father's wrath by speaking such, but you will be missed." Then, hastily, as a whisper: "I will miss you."

The skies rumbled then, but at a distance where massive thunderheads formed several hundred feet from shore.

Laurel fought to get her hand back from Mira, the woman's strength disturbingly more powerful than Laurel would have granted. *She's a damn Fate what do you expect!?* "Let go of me," Laurel found her other hand trapped within Makaisi's grip.

Clouds gathered over Paul's lighthouse, brief flashes of white lightning volleying between the thick gray masses.

The two women escorted her toward the lighthouse.

"You will hear our song no more," Mira spoke quickly but hesitantly as if searching for a special tool to make just the right shape in the grain of her words. "You have...moved us." She nodded contentedly, smiling at Makaisi who scowled back.

"I don't want to go to the lighthouse," she spit the words out trying to pull away from the sisters. *Do they know I know?* She wondered and then regretted the thought because what if that was all it took? Paul had said something about them messing with his Threads—damnit, she had to focus, she had to keep up with what was happening.

"Oh, my *oraios*," Mira's voice creaked. "We are only bringing you home."

Laurel watched the age lines around Mira's eyes flex and bow. "Bullshit. You're lying to me—that's what you do, you three. You twist and tie and you...Let go of my hands!" Laurel knew that if she didn't take hold of the pendant again something bad was going to happen.

Makaisi clicked her tongue and toyed with strands of Laurel's hair that had pulled free of the shells and braids. "But it is good. It is as it should be for you. For us." Mira turned to smile at her sister, showing Laurel an array of misshapen yellowed and stained teeth.

"It is happening too quickly, sister." Mira's eyes seemed moist but Laurel could not focus, she felt intoxicated.

Paul. Poseidon. She repeated his names over and over quickly trying to keep her focus.

"The Riders stand in the froth, they are eager to finish their dance." Makaisi adjusted the ornate dark brown shawl wrapped around her narrow shoulders. The pattern: an image of hundreds of interwoven spider webs connecting the braided hems of the shawl drawn across her slight back.

"I know who you are," Laurel said. "You can't make me go home—I don't want to go." She said coldly, the haziness in her thoughts dissipated momentarily. "You're the sisters of Fate, the cutter, the measurer—" Makaisi toyed with the air around Laurel and her thoughts jumbled again. "Damnit, stop doing that!"

"You see and then you do not; that is the way of it." Mira spoke gently, sadly.

Laurel seized the moment and ripped her hand away from Mira.

"You mustn't!" Makaisi's voice screeched like a record needle kicked across an old 45. "Sister! Stop her!"

Laurel took hold of the pendant and immediately felt Paul's presence—not out near the shallop but all around her and in everything. *I don't know how this works,* her thoughts gained footing and she skimmed through fragments of myth trying to preen out one that might grant her an edge over the sisters.

"Daughter of Nash, you mustn't interfere with the Weave!" Makaisi's voice cracked as she tried to pry Laurel's fingers off the pendant.

"You cannot win—your dance here is at an end; let us see you on your way." Mira spoke soothingly, though she could not hide the strain in her voice. The gnarls and knots of

Mira's face shifted quickly between smiles and grimaces as she struggled with Laurel. "We are sorry for it to be this way —to return you this way." More grunts and struggling and then Mira whispered: "It is not a unanimous effort."

"Sister!" Makaisi's lithe form abruptly towered over Mira and Laurel found herself suddenly free.

"Both of you can go to hell!" Laurel ran from them, shouting for Old Poppa.

They grabbed at her, Mira's fat hands slapping at Laurel's back, Makaisi's nails digging into Laurel's scalp. The three women fell; Laurel's hand broke contact with the pendant. She felt their hands grabbing clothing and hair and then she felt them touching something inside.

It felt like a piano wire connected to the base of her skull was being hammered by a three year old on the ivories.

The sister's invisible touches had breached whatever defenses Paul had erected in the lighthouse. The piano wire thrummed setting off more vibrations across her Threads unleashing a barrage of memories:

Dad's funeral. Drinking herself into a stupor every night for weeks. Getting approval for a sabbatical from CFCC. Selling Dad's house the same day she found his floatplan and journal. Drinking away an entire weekend then trying to sell his ship.

Crying, drinking, anger, destruction and then submission.

Boarding *The Ghost* with every intent of following Dad's floatplan by sailing to Greece alone. The peace of the ocean broken by the storm, losing the ship. Floating forever. And then the green flash and the strange blind man.

Finally Paul.

"STOP!" she screamed and tore away from them.

Makaisi's husky laugh sickened her. "She doesn't care for the plucking of her Threads."

Laurel slapped Makaisi. The shock set the woman back two paces, Mira did not move at all. "If you ever do that to me again I will choke you with your damn Threads."

A beat of silence and then she heard Old Poppa's voice shouting, "Away from her witches!" He appeared beside her shouting at the sisters in Greek.

The air grew hot around her, her vision shifted and the pungent aroma of oranges nearly sent her puking. She felt a cold hand closing around the back of her neck and she knew without seeing that Mathropos had finally come to the party.

"And what would you do to the Keeper of the Threads, little fin, hmmm?" Mathropos spoke her father's pet name for her in a sickening sing-song voice.

Laurel reached for the pendant but Mira and Makaisi held her arms back.

"Let's see what happens if I tuck this dark strand back into place, shall we?" Mathropos pushed a finger into the back of Laurel's head and suddenly she was sitting in her apartment talking on the phone to her father.

Laurel?

"No, please...please stop oh God, please, please don't make me remember this, please don't make me remember this, please don't!" The hand of the Keeper forced Laurel to her knees in the sand.

Laurel, can you come to Hatteras tonight? I can't find my glasses and there's a storm coming. The ship is listing and I can't find my glasses....

Dad, I've got a huge research assignment planned—
It's ok, honey. I just can't...I can't find my glasses.
Dad?

...

Daddy?

"Please stop...I couldn't go...just, make it stop...."

"Is that what you wish, daughter of Nash?" Mathropos' voice, lyrical yet taut, drifted through the painful memory to her ears.

"Yes. I can't do it again; please I don't want to lose him again." Laurel waited. She knew the Keeper was stronger, smarter. All she had to do was get hold of the pendant.

Mathropos hoisted her up, brushed sand from her chiton, and set her on two feet again.

"I have the power to honor your wishes, daughter of Nash." Mathropos grinned and the world around them stopped.

EIGHT

"It would have been better for you to have not been here at all, Daughter of Nash. A shame that I cannot retie those strings any differently." Mathropos spoke in Greek and English somehow. And somehow, they were moving, walking Laurel supposed, although she wasn't making any effort to walk. The world had not yet restarted. Old Poppa stood frozen between the sisters who were unaffected by the stoppage of time.

In her head, Laurel wailed for Paul, resisting every fiber of her being to call him Poseidon. *I can't yet...no, not yet... they have to be the same man, right?* Elsewhere in her thoughts she recalled pages of text in mythology books from Thomas Bullfinch to Edith Hamilton and always the Fates were conniving, mischievous, self-serving witches. And while these three certainly fit that bill, Mathropos was all that and more. Darker, older, far more sinister.

"I'm sorry for your loss," Mira's driftwood hands worked themselves over and over, her voice carried a deep groan; an old oak fighting an even older wind. "I wonder if perhaps we might not have been frien—"

"Stifle your tongue, *sister*." Cold words darted from Mathropos and Mira shriveled back. "Your historic stupidity under the guise of *wondering* has angered Father and *me* once too often."

Mira wilted back, still holding Laurel's left hand, petting it.

Makaisi carried Laurel's right hand as it were tainted; the taller sister cast Mira a sour glare.

"You should never have come, child. You should have allowed us to escort you back the moment you set foot on this island. I have sacrificed too much to keep Olympos free from Earthsider vermin. I am the *Keeper,* child—you cannot best me." Mathropos spoke like a teacher who hated her students. "Now, because of you and *Paul Okeanos* all of this will mean *nothing*." Like an asp with lips, she pronounced each word carefully, still in that double-speak of Greek and English and somehow, Laurel understood both. The air in front of Laurel puckered as Mathropos glided before of her.

"I can stop your pains, remove the memories too if you wish, Daughter of Nash, but you can fight us no longer." The ashen-faced Keeper grinned, showing long white teeth in a thin lipped mouth.

Laurel's mind reeled trying to take in the truth but at the same time repel the memories of abandoning her father. "I don't know why you're doing this...I didn't come here to ruin *anything*!? I've done nothing wrong." But Laurel knew she had. Like knowing that a thunderstorm approaches miles off...like Dad knowing the hidden shoals. Laurel sensed she had upset a hidden balance. *Four days, Athena's island, the Allagi.*

Poseidon.

Laurel swallowed back her fears, tried to stifle the simmering anger at Paul for setting her in the middle of all this. *He tried to explain*, she reminded herself—*bound by the laws of this land blah blah*—it was the same crap every man tried throwing at a woman when they know they've screwed up. God of Olympos or not, Paul had some explaining to do.

Mathropos raised her arms and the heavily embroidered shawl fell back showing unnaturally tight skin mottled by white, brown and drab-green age spots. Thick purple veins squirmed and twisted beneath her skin, making it undulate and crawl like snakes in a burlap sack. Mathropos placed her fingers on either side of Laurel's face. They burned and cooled as they slipped over her cheeks and around her neck.

"Whatever you're gonna do, you better make sure it works. Because I'm gonna kick your ass all over this beach." She braced herself for the fight; she'd seen enough hanging out with Coasties—Dad had taught her more than how to handle herself on the water.

Mathropos grinned and lifted Laurel one inch off the ground and six inches closer to her awful face. The flesh covering the Keeper's head appeared slightly out of place as if she'd decided at the last moment to put on someone else's skin. The folds and crevices about her mouth and eyes reminded Laurel of a forgotten statue; that of a gargoyle. The veins moved there too. The odor of oranges grew rotten.

"Do not cast your eyes upon me with disgust. *This is your doing.* Yours and *his*...your Paul Okeanos. My sisters and I are beyond weary trying to reweave what you and he took limitless merriment in undoing. I promise you this, Daughter of Nash: after tonight there will be no more Earthsider's tampering with the Weave."

"Put me down."

"You are not in a position to—"

Laurel ripped her arms away from the flanking sisters and put both hands on Mathropos, digging her nails in deeply—all the way in to the silty, coral-like flesh of her face. "I said put me down!" She raked her nails up and back.

"*Aaaiiyah!*" the old woman wailed and released Laurel, dropping her in a heap to the sand.

Laurel did not hesitate; she pushed off with her feet and ran out of the pocket the sisters had formed around her.

"You cannot run from this, Daughter of Nash." Impossibly, Mathropos stood before her in the darkness. Ugly red trails painted her face now and Laurel grinned at her.

"I know what you are, Keeper. You and your sisters don't frighten me. I may not know everything, but I do know this: Right now: You're on the losing team. So let me tell you something this Daughter of Nash learned from Mr. Nash himself, *if you're gonna fight girl, you're gonna have to take a hit.*" Laurel swung at Mathropos but the woman was amazingly swift, dodging down and back throwing Laurel off balance.

She recovered quickly. "Not too bad for an old bitch. Did you think I was some kinda pushover because I'm not from here?"

"It matters not. We can no longer tolerate this dance." Mathropos tilted her head like a bird listening for worms. When she grinned, Laurel swallowed hard.

"Listen crypt-keeper—I'm going to get off this island. I'm going to figure out how to stop whatever the hell is wrong with this place. And I'm going to find Paul and then I'm going home."

Mathropos tilted her head up slightly and a narrow grin pulled apart the out-of-place-lips of her face. "To the light-house? Or back to Hatteras, North Carolina?"

From the Keeper's mouth Hatteras came out *Hat-ter-us*. Laurel was shaking and trying very hard to hide it. She knew her father would be proud for mustering the backbone to stand up to the Keeper but she wasn't sure she couldn't keep up the act. *Where's Old Poppa? Ulgos?* All she needed was a chance to grab the pendant or run or both. She opted for stalling.

"Yeah, home to the lighthouse—I've got nothing in *Hat*-teras. I just want to be alone. In the lighthouse." Laurel sensed that the world was restarting, all the elements had begun to fade back into their original positions; colors, noises, even the smell of the ocean.

"Is *that* what this is all about?" Mathropos laughed. It was a gurgling trill that covered Laurel in goosebumps. "Oh, Child, my apologies. Be about it then." She returned her head to its original position, the skin on her face now properly aligned perhaps even more youthful.

And like a stage curtain rising, the air, color, and noise of the island fell back into the world leaving Laurel but a few paces from the base of her haven. The sisters stood at a distance near their hut, Mira and Makaisi embracing, Mathropos tousling the hair of Amynta's twins as the boys stood placidly watching.

For a few moments, Laurel still felt piano wires thrumming throughout her body.

"There you are, Poet." Old Poppa placed a wide and heavy hand on her shoulder, shaking her gently. "The nap did you well; there is color in your face again."

"Damnit," Laurel held her emotions in check, kept her face serene. She could not let the sisters know she knew. They had manipulated the present, shifted time and placed her back a few hours. She didn't know if any of the others had been affected. There would be no way for her to find out without revealing herself to the Fates. "Damnit," she cursed again.

Strangely, the Fates were now involved in a scratch game

of soccer with the twins. Overhead, the sun had just started to make its descent into the ocean. Nearby, the tables were being erected and food placed out for the mourners.

"Ulgos worries about you, Poet. He fears you have lost your way." Old Poppa stepped in front of her and placed his sea-salted hands on her face the same way her dad had done many times. "You are a'pretty, Laurel. What does Mira call you? Yes, *oraios*. It fits. Always do you remind me of blossoms. Do not let them wilt you. These folk here...they are stuck. You are not."

"You're right", she whispered. "Sorta. Old Poppa, I know. I know what this place is I know where I'm supposed to go but I can't let the sisters know. Help me." To emphasize her point she tapped the aegis.

Around her, mourners talked, the virgins sang, and the bare-chested men prepared to carry Paul's body out into the ocean. The Fates clearly had more power than any of the myths had ever attributed to them. But they were not perfect; they'd left her Threads intact. It had to be because of Paul. *Poseidon!* She would never get used to calling him that.

The old man's face did not change but his voice hardened. "Aye, Poet. Then it has begun. Ulgos will be with us shortly, we must tread carefully else the witches will Remove you all together, despite the consequences."

"I'm guessing Removing someone is dangerous, and probably not something I can come back from."

"None can return from *Afairó*," Ulgos intoned gravely.

Laurel pursed her lips, casting an eye toward the suspiciously distracted sisters. "I need to get off this island, Old Poppa. I have to get to...to Athena." It was easier to say but not any easier to believe. *Time and distance*, Paul had said to her.

"We shall aid you in your exodus, Poet; I give you my oath by the blood of my fathers before me as they have to Poseidon so too shall I be yours in service." He knelt, kissed her hand and stood.

"Thank you, Old Poppa. I...this is..."

He put a hand to her lips. "You need not explain. It is best you keep it for yourself, for now. Perhaps, upon another island, another time, you can share your Earthsider stories with me. For now, wait here. Be wary of the sisters, Poet. Be wary."

Laurel hugged him and then he was gone, moving away quickly. She traced her toes through the sands trying to appear somber, alone but all the while keeping an eye on the sisters.

And suddenly she was among them or they had already surrounded her. *Be still, be ready* she steeled herself.

"All is right with the Weave," Makaisi hummed lightly.

"It hasn't settled yet, sister; we mustn't upset her Threads if—" Mira started but Mathropos cut her off.

"Cease your nattering you insipid old fools. Child, you seem perplexed. What plagues you?" Her voice no longer had the doubling of English and Greek, her skin had returned to a healthy youthful vigor. But the Keeper still exuded a darkness older than anything Laurel had ever encountered.

"Sister, she has not embraced the new pattern fully yet— you are frightening her." Mira stepped timidly into view, a wide but faulty grin bridging her chubby cheeks.

The Keeper cracked Mira sharply on the top of her head.

Laurel played the doe in their presence. But she desperately wanted to take hold of the pendant to recharge her connection with Paul—Poseidon. She could not, though, without risking the wrath of the Fates.

"Did you hear me, Daughter of Nash? It is not so strange a question. You need only give consent and then we'll burn off the frayed ends of these threads and put the Weave right again. So, I ask again: May I aid you in your return?" Mathropos' hands unraveled themselves from around Laurel's arm.

"I think I'll stay...pay my respects." Laurel moved carefully, purposefully slow. Whatever power the Fates wielded could not control her completely. They needed her consent in order to make it work.

Mathropos caught her elbow and whirled her around, her eyes hard and hot, their faces close to touching.

"Girl! Do not make me reweave this again; I've not the patience for it! We are upon the lighthouse, we can set *all of this* as it should be." She gestured flippantly in the direction of the black and white spire. The ancient woman's voice resonated with whispers of other conversations. "*See?* Now give your consent." Mathropos plucked at the air, twirled her fingers, criss-crossing them as if she were frantically knitting.

"Don't play the game with me, Keeper." Laurel leaned in so close her lips nearly brushed against Mathropos' cheek. In the woman's face, she saw minute, blacks tendrils writhing beneath her skin. "I know what you are—you can't mess with my Threads anymore." She laid both hands over the pendant and stepped back.

A barely audible *twick* cut the air between her and Mathropos. Something had broken and the result filled the old woman's dark eyes with white, the movement of tendrils beneath her flesh riotous. Like oil beneath a cloth, the mottling seeped back into her skin.

Everything happened at once.

Old Poppa shouted curses in Greek.

Ulgos shoved between Mira and Makaisi and picked up Mathropos, tossing her down the beach like a discarded robe.

"Eeeeiiiaarrh! Bastard you will regr—*gugnh!*" the woman landed solidly on her head, the weight of her body twisting her neck at an unnatural angle.

"Sister!" Mira and Makasai screeched simultaneously.

"It is good to see you again, my friends." Laurel hugged both men.

"The witches will recover swiftly, we've no time," Old Poppa grunted his words, his face red and raining sweat.

"The Angler has arrived, father." Ulgos swept Laurel off her feet effortlessly.

"Put her upon the ship, I will hold the witches back as long as I can." Old Poppa squeezed Laurel's hand to his chest. "Trust the Angler, Poet—his debt to Poseidon is greater than any within Olympos."

"Ulgos, no! Wait!" she implored, but he was already trotting to the shoreline.

"Put her aboard. Stop for nothing," the old man called after them. "This is the only way, Poet. Forgive us." The sisters had regrouped around Old Poppa but now a few of the mourners stood with him as well.

"Ulgos, go back—we can't leave him." Laurel held on as Ulgos picked up speed.

"He has danced with the Fates before; it is they who should be wary." Ulgos carried her to the docks just west of the lighthouse where a black ship awaited.

"Is Paul dead?" she let Ulgos set her down then took his face in her hands.

He did not answer.

"Ulgos, I need something—I don't know what's out there;

hell I don't know a damn thing about this Olympos except for Paul. Is he *really* dead?"

Ulgos looked up at the lighthouse and then back to Laurel. "I do not know if you will find Paul Okeanos at the end of your journey. I am sorry."

Behind them came Makaisi wailing like a banshee.

Ulgos grabbed Laurel again, handling her like a sack of potatoes. He ran down the docks, his wide feet thundering over the planks. Shouts of terror and wails of fear erupted all around. Without hesitation or even a warning, Ulgos tossed Laurel from the docks onto the deck of the ship.

And then the sisters took him.

NINE

"Olympos will never be the same," Amynta whispered as she ascended the spiral staircase of the lighthouse. The spire did not have its life any more, of that she was certain; and it startled her that she felt so strongly about an Earthsider.

Her doubts aside, Laurel Nash had certainly brought a vibrancy to Lord Poseidon.

Enough to keep him whole in death? She quickly brushed away the thought, for surely Lord Poseidon would not enter into such a gambit without knowing all possible outcomes. Just the same, Amynta did not know the gods' tolerance for such tragedies. None of them had ever died before, to her knowledge. She steeled her thoughts from further tangents, remonstrating herself for any doubt. "I believe," she whispered. She hurried along the steps caught up in her convictions so deeply that she only saw the shadow of the woman descending upon her.

"Filthy little vixen!" spittle flew from Makaisi's teeth, spattering Amynta's face.

Amynta moved swiftly, jumping high and grabbing the edge of the closest protruding stone. Scrambling more than climbing, she managed to reach the landing of her master's sanctum faster than Makaisi could follow. The anteroom resembled the pilot house of a ship. *I believe I believe* she admonished herself, moving as fast as she could for she had a task to complete for Lord Poseidon and would not be deterred by—

"You are quick, little *defender* but I see where you mean to go before you go!" Makaisi pulled herself through the air as if climbing hidden ropes and dropped ahead of Amynta so quickly she could not stop her forward momentum.

Amynta crashed into the Sister who caught her by the throat and hair. "Curse you *Krino!* You cannot harm me else you break your own *laws!*"

Makaisi snarled and threw Amynta into a short table, the force rolling her over it and against the whitewashed walls. "Do not call me by that foul name!"

Amynta tasted blood in her mouth but pulled herself up to face Makaisi...*Krino*, the Judge. "Why? Is that not the task with which The Keeper has charged you?"

"Bah! You are merely your master's defender, *Amynta!* I am Makaisi, and *only* Makaisi. And you will tell me the Earthsider's destination or I will find the means to bend your Weave and make your suffering eternal." Makaisi stepped face to face with Amynta, leaving her no escape but through the shuttered windows to her left.

I believe, she repeated again, tasting the fetid breath of the Sister. Amynta believed her, for though the Fates were bound by laws which prevented them from directly harming any subject of a god, these did not prevent them from metering out torment.

It was then that the boy blasted through the shuttered window and directly into the two women, carrying them across the landing to the edge of the stairway.

Amynta seized the moment of distraction, extracting herself from the pile and shoving Makaisi down the spiral staircase. Their laws, blessedly, did not apply to Amynta.

"I am terribly sorry for the insolence...invasion...intrusion?" the boy seemed as dazed as the Sister who struggled to pull herself from the floor.

"Silence boy! Help me rid the lighthouse of her!" Amynta leapt down several steps, landing with a harsh crunch of her right ankle. Makaisi sneered as she gathered her wits.

The boy did not hesitate, moving more swiftly than Amynta imagined possible, appearing behind the Fate. He slid his arms up behind her, securing the woman's arms though she still tried biting at him, gnashing her teeth dreadfully close to the boy's face.

"Boy, I will violate *every law* if you do not release me!" Makaisi paused, her smile spreading wider than a normal mouth would allow. "And I will not give you the same pleasure of removal I gave your mother, *child*, I...will simply...*kill* you!" The invisible ropes briefly appeared around Makaisi, each a different coarseness, color, and size. The Fate struggled to free herself from the boy's grasp and soon would if Amynta did not act.

"That's a tad harsh, I just got here." His whimsical smile did nothing to settle the Sister nor hide the fear flashing through his eyes.

"You are bound, *Krino*...you cannot harm us; Lord Poseidon will—"

"*Lord Poseidon is dead!*" Makaisi ripped away from the boy, elevating herself above them as a monkey might through low hanging branches.

Amynta pulled the boy close to her, surprised Lord Poseidon had enlisted his aid given the damage his father had caused during the war. But then, Daedalus had certainly paid a blood debt, so perhaps she should not be so surprised to see Icarus.

"I'm sorry," the boy whispered as his wings nervously fluttered against his back.

"Believe, boy...that is all I ask of you." Amynta stood her ground and waited for Makaisi to attack.

TEN

Mathropos adjusted her head, the bones in her neck grinding against one another like cinderblocks. She had faced many adversaries, and had certainly taken far more severe damage.

But never for the sake of an *Earthsider*.

If her skin were not already crawling from the massive volume of Threads she held, it certainly would now out of consequence. She watched the undulating fibers align themselves along her arm, marveling at the alluring entropy their movement created beneath her flesh. *You carry too much*, she scolded herself gently. A necessary sacrifice for the betterment of Olympos; without the Threads she could not possibly hope to wield the *Dunamis* or affect the proper changes in Zeus or—

She ceased her thinking to concentrate on recovering the Earthsider.

The beach, empty now except for a few gulls and the remains of the funerary accoutrements, always made her think of futility. With every step, the sands shifted beneath your feet forcing you to continuously readjust your stance. Nothing like the Threads. Each strand could be measured, decisively; each strand had its purpose, each strand had a finite existence. Sand and water possessed a deceptive fluidity she found repulsive. She would be quite pleased to be done with this business and be off Poseidon's island permanently.

Mathropos took another moment to brush the recalcitrant sands from her robes and found a stray Thread near her left foot. She held it aloft and watched it willowing in the ocean breeze. To her, the Thread held choices, distinct, measureable, definable choices. Even as she pushed the wayward strand into her right eye where it belonged, she knew to whom the filament once belonged and at what cost the previous owner paid to live without it.

She smiled, satisfied, almost gleeful, really, for the Law cannot be broken. Ever. And she, of all Olympos' denizens, could truthfully admit she had never broken a single Law. *Any ward of any god shall na'er fall to harm or death at the hands of the Fates lest she herself be willing to suffer twenty-fold the same.*

Mathropos had certainly suffered.

I have suffered a thousand-fold and will suffer more to bring the Earthsider's Threads to truncation. The Threads roiled within her and she could not allow them to gain control again. *I am the Keeper!* She bore down on the thought until the filaments of mortals' fate returned to more slothful undulations.

She walked to the lighthouse in search of her sisters. Stupid Mira would most likely be nursing her thin hide in their huts while Makaisi had surprisingly *not* yet set fire to the lighthouse. To be burdened by such insipid siblings only added to her suffering and solidified her martyrdom. In the end, Zeus and all the gods would thank her for severing what remained of the Connection to Earthside. Their Threads, after all, gave her no strength, provided only mild entertainment but ultimately tainted the woof and weft of the Grand Weave, the *Theosophane*.

Laurel Nash must be Removed. The cost, she knew, would challenge the Law and she would certainly risk Father's wrath, but surely her suffering would account for something?

Time ebbed on, however, and of that she had little to spare. She lamented the old ways, for it seemed then that was all she did have time to do: *think*. She rechecked the Threads, content that the mass was under control and proceeded toward the lighthouse in earnest.

"Mira will need to stay her tongue," the Keeper muttered to herself, growing increasingly frustrated with every step she took through the sands. "Makaisi has shown promising growth of late; a fierceness to be reckoned with." She felt eyes upon her, read the Threads and knew each choice to come, every decision ever made, what possibilities lay ahead along the watchers' Fate. The old man and his son, perhaps several other of Poseidon's useless wards. No matter. Let them watch. For along the Threads radiated the dark fear she had painstakingly wound into many of them. Otherwise she could not have orchestrated Poseidon's death.

Mathropos reached the base of the lighthouse and heard the cacophony of crashes, shouts, and chaos from above as she opened the door. It took her a moment to glide up the steps, an effort which grew increasingly more taxing with every Thread she assimilated, and placed herself between Makaisi and the woman—Poseidon's annoying Oikonomos—and the winged-boy.

"Stop this!" she commanded them, their decisions, choices, and outcomes fanned out before her like so many playing cards. "I do not have time for this. Nor do you, sister!"

Makaisi seethed but retracted her talons, or rather, her gavel. Mathropos had to be patient. Mira would be the first, she had decided that long ago before embarking upon this path. But to wield the Thread *and* the Gavel? *Focus woman!* She felt the Threads churning again, they'd become more aggressive as of late. "How dare you," she hissed at Makaisi. "You know the Law, sister." *There, better...* focused...*and safe.*

"They know where the Earthsider travels, sister." Makaisi spoke coldly, oblivious to the internal maelstrom raging within Mathropos.

"Ahhh, and have they shared this morsel with you?" Mathropos watched the boy and this woman—why could she not glean her name?—cataloguing their Threads. This worried her unexpectedly.

"No. I have not harmed them nor did I intend to; I came only to gather information."

"Lies," the woman bleated. Mathropos listened to the Threads for the woman's name but no answer came.

The boy remained pale with fear, his wings quivering. Mathropos hid her alarm; if Icarus had become involved with Poseidon that meant Daedulus would be meddling as well. She had to regain focus. Perhaps if she consumed more Threads....

"Silence!" she spat; the Threads riled up and eager. "You should have called for me, sister. You needn't threaten them to gain what we seek."

"Aye...you were...occupied." The sarcasm fractured her sister's words.

To be dealt with later, she thrummed her sister's Weave with the thought and Makaisi's eyes narrowed, darkened.

She knew the wrong she'd committed and thrummed back: *do not tell Father*.

Mathropos smiled. "I see your choices, I know your decisions *before* you do. Ah! See, there, right beside your hope of fleeing without consequence—which I might add isn't likely. Oh how marvelous to witness the shifting Pattern of your Fate! It's remarkable, wouldn't you agree, sister?"

Makaisi moved closer to Mathropos, practically stroking her arm in search of sympathy. Perhaps it would be her to go first; only minor adjustments would need to be made. She risked feeling along that darkest most-hidden of strands and saw that it was possible if she acted now.

"Isn't he the one, sister?" Mathropos began.

"Aye...son of the Master Inventor." Makaisi continued, discreetly petting Mathropos' arm.

"'Tis a shame about your mother, boy; she needn't have been dealt with so harshly but then that sort of thing is in your blood, isn't it?" Mathropos waited for that subtle shift... the one that said—AH! Yes, there it is. She quickly tied off that tiny filament, anchoring it to the hidden strand, satisfaction now sedating the Threads completely.

"I know where the Earthsider travels, sister. We have matters to attend to. Where is your fat shadow?" Mathropos glared at the woman—*what is her name!?*

"Where else? She cowers in the huts waiting to jump at your next command. Useless."

"Be at ease, sister; come. You have been most helpful, Icarus and..." she paused certain that she should have known the woman's name, disturbed that she could not pull it from her Threads. "Amynta." At last! Neither of them seemed to notice the delay and it was for the best. She could not have it be known the Keeper might not be in complete control.

"You are no longer welcome upon this isle." Amynta growled at the sisters.

"A bit of fire in you, eh? Be careful woman. Your Weave portends great ache for your twins." Mathropos remembered now; this woman had become Poseidon's nursemaid, the Earthsider's nanny—*why did I not know this immediately?*—during the course of the last year. There was something here, something in this lighthouse....

"Shall we go, sister?" Makaisi said, breaking her thoughts.

"Indeed. We must retrieve the Earthsider before she reaches," she paused, smiled at the boy and Amynta and then finished, "Athena's island. It is likely that wretched Angler will be ferrying her. Come."

Mathropos deftly plucked her way along the Threads Makaisi used to descend the lighthouse, troubled by what had happened above. She would need to find more strands; surely she could retain more. *I am the Keeper, after all.*

ELEVEN

The olive-skinned man tilted his head left and right in a slow metronome with the gently rocking ship as he watched Laurel. She wasn't sure if she should jump up and attack him or remain still.

She wasn't sure of much, truthfully.

His pupil-less eyes hovered in his head like dull opals, encrusted by the heavy folds of his eyelids and hooded by bushy bronze eyebrows. A rudder-like nose cast a thick shadow over thin, cracked and bloodied lips that moved in rhythm with the waves lapping the sides of the ship. His shaven head continued its rolling bob.

"I'm thirsty," she croaked. Her throat hurt, her body hurt more. Overhead, a brilliant ochre sun drifted lazily just above the horizon in the west. Laurel lay still, marveling at the sun as it toyed with the ocean, slipping down just close enough for the waters to feel its heat and then up again with a chuckle.

The ship danced with the waves too, curtsying gracefully despite the aggressive embrace of the ocean around it. Broad umber sails billowed out from the center mast with every gust of wind, yet the ship seemed reluctant to move as quickly as the winds encouraged.   Every few moments the genoa snapped to attention so strongly it shuddered the mast.

"Close reach?" Laurel asked hoarsely.

"In th'irons. Water. Over there." The man moved closer, out of the shadow of the mast, his weather-beaten body taut as a rhumb line. A small copse of black and white hairs gathered at his sternum cresting the top of a ragged rake of a scar that traveled the length of his body, disappearing below the belt line.

Laurel still did not move her head or torso to reach the water. Her left hand caught the handle of a pewter decanter and brought it to her lips. A cold shock rushed into her, reawakening her limbs and digits and flushing out more aches.

Her first undiluted thought: *I've been on this ship before.*

She recognized the murky color of the sails, the odd bowl-shape of the hull, the faded mural of an immense battle painted upon the forlorn decking.   Men and monsters clashing at sea painted from aft to stern centered on a figure too faded to discern, standing in the shadow of the main mast.

And of course the blind Angler. A vague recognition surfaced of him too.

"Ay-yuh," he nodded at her as if acknowledging the realization.

Laurel closed her eyes and took hold of the silver owl hanging around her neck. *Paul, where are you?* She felt him, but only on the periphery of this elusive connection. She dared not call out to him as Poseidon for fear he would respond.

Poseidon. The word felt heavy in her thoughts, heaviest of all in fact. Nothing of what Mathropos and the Fates had done to her compared to acclimating herself to the fact that she had been intimate with a god. *Just say it*, she chided. *Say the words you're feeling.* I love Poseidon.

Nope.

Too weird.

I love Paul Okeanos. Better. But Paul was dead and the shimmery sterling wall presently occupying her brain seemed to be doing a pretty damn good job of allowing her to think about anything but the present. Nonetheless, swimming within the argent depths, were shadows of massive leviathans: Olympians are real, the Fates are real—and quite insidious—and she had genuinely failed her father.

That last one hovered too close to the surface for her. Damn you, Mathropos.

Enough time and distance, Paul had assured her, *and you should recover enough.* She wanted to believe that; she was desperate to avoid unraveling now. Laurel made a quick diagnostic of her internal-self. Her bones resonated with warnings. Much like when she knew Dad had died.

Mathropos' manipulations of her memories flash-fired through her, dominated by that neglected, overwhelming solitary feeling she was certain her father had felt. *Because of me. All I had to do was drive three hours up the coast.* Truth was, she had ignored her bones—*it's cuz they're made of salt girl and they know what the ocean knows* Dad always told her. She would not make the same mistake again.

For now, Laurel decided to force her bones into silence, so she could take stock of where she was, what to do—she cast a side glance at the blind angler—and figure out his role in this crazy adventure.

As if on cue, the Angler walked by, methodical in his cadence; his bare feet *skiff-skiffing* in rhythm to the rolling dance of the ship. He wore salt-stained and tattered leggings that might once have been red, an intricately woven multi-colored hemp belt, and an array of bracelets and baubles up the length of his left forearm. In his left ear, three gold hoops sparkled in the fading sunlight; a single fat copper hoop dangled from his right. He took hold of a wayward batten, and resecured it deftly. The movement of his nimble fingers reminded her of the sisters and instantly, her guard went up.

"Who are you?" she managed to hoist herself up on both elbows. Her sunburned, unshaven legs poked out from beneath a stained gray shift which clung to her breasts and back. "Awesome. I might as well be naked. What happened to my chiton? And where's the island? How close are we to...Athena...oh God...why does my body hurt?"

The Angler paid her no heed.

"Great. Blind *and* deaf. Where are we?"

"Trutina," the Angler's voice came from below.

"Is that where we are or your name? What are you doing over there? Hey!" Laurel paused, waited. No answer. She examined the ship, finding vague elements that might be familiar. A year had passed, so much had happened in that year. Hell, so much had happened in...in...she could not place a timestamp on it. "What day is it? How much time has passed since Ulgos threw me aboard?"

No reply except for the shuffling and random noises emanating from below.

"Hey! I said—"

"I am Trutina. You are aboard my ship, *The Balance*." The Angler stood over her, his face expressionless, even gaunt. His narrow, sinewy arms reached down and scooped her up to a sitting position.

"Whoa buddy, let's not get too friendly! Okay, you're gonna get punched if you keep—" but she was up on her feet, albeit unsteadily, and Trutina's hands were shackles on her wrists as he held her in place.

"See." He chanted in her ear. His breath came like a hot desert wind reeking of onions and fish. Laurel's vision rolled but not with the dance of the ship.

"*See*," The Angler's word coddled and cajoled her.

"I'm going to be sick. I mean it—I...am...going to puke." Laurel wanted to drop to her knees but Trutina wouldn't allow her. "Please, I don't think I have my sea-legs yet. Just give me a minute to.... Oh. My. God."

Trutina did not answer; instead he turned her body to face the western sky where the sun still teased the horizon. She expected to see an endless blue carpet of ocean.

Instead she stared at a magnificent mottled black and azure reef out of which jutted blades of gray, weathered coral, like misshapen vertebrae.   And where the waters lapped at its base, fist-sized, white, pink, and chartreuse sea-shells made a twisting trail back and forth along the body of the reef.   Abandoned treasures crusted the entire reef: a sextant, mismatched boots, a water-logged book, barnacle crusted planks, cups, bowls, cutlery—she could not take it all in.

"I've never seen anything like it." Indeed, she had swum the Great Barrier Reef, had explored more than a few wrecks just outside of the Diamond Shoals but this surpassed them all. "It's breathtaking." She felt small in the shadow of the massive reef, rising two to four feet in some sections and as wide as Trutina's boat for as far as she could see in either direction. Gulls and other birds filled the air with their discordant cries, assaulting the reef in search of easy prey. The waves never ceased their continuous conversation with one another. *The Balance* herself murmured and creaked in the secret language of wooden ships.

She was certain that if Trutina weren't holding her she would have collapsed.

"Ay-yuh," the Angler spoke evenly, "You see *Yfalos*...The Reef. Here is where I and you became acquainted."

"I don't remember." Bile filled her mouth and she ripped herself away from Trutina, falling to the railing and releasing the contents of her stomach.

"No surprise," he left her there in her misery, returning to whatever menial task her questions had interrupted before. "Thirteen months have passed since I and you made our first voyage."

"Oh..." She vomited again. "You...oh God..." she could not hold herself upright and it seemed she would never stop puking. Thirteen months. "Time...*gahh*...and distance," she managed at last but did not lift herself up from the railing. *What have I missed back home?* It didn't matter. What she'd experienced here mattered. She didn't like the number thirteen though; it was easier to digest if she thought of it as about a year. Laurel spit more bile from her mouth and then sat heavily beside the rail, still holding on. "How long have I been aboard *The Balance*, this time?"

"The first day ends soon." Trutina continued about his business, oblivious to Laurel's turmoil.

"Oh hell, I'm gonna puke again." Laurel braced herself but only dry heaves wracked her this time.

"I have not the answers you seek. But it is within my power to deliver you where you wish to go. Perhaps to those answers. Perhaps to others. If you wish it." He approached her again holding a leafy green eggroll-thing.

"Oh my God, you're insane! I can't eat that. Have you looked in the water at what came out of my mouth?" She wanted answers, but more than anything she wanted Paul. She wanted the comfort he could give her without saying a word; she wanted the balance he provided simply by touching her skin. "Can you take me to Paul?"

"It is not for you to eat." Trutina's long fingered hands unrolled the eggroll-thing swiftly and he wiped her face delicately. Mint and cinnamon drifted into her mouth, and some other aroma she couldn't place immediately—almost like Pepto Bismol. Trutina cleaned her without haste, when he finished he tossed the waste into the ocean.

Though the concoction did not eliminate her queasiness all together, it did immediately remove the foul odor. She felt like she could stand up without falling down at least. Trutina disappeared below decks again. Laurel sighed and waited.

The *Balance* moaned desperately, eager to be free of her anchor. Laurel closed her eyes and listened. *Can you hear her, Laurel? She's lonely for the sea; feel that, lil'fin, how she pulls at th'anchor? A moored ship knows you've caught her and if you hold still you'll know which way she's wantin' to go.*

"I miss you Dad." She whispered to the ocean. Gulls cried back to her: *min-ih MY-nah* and waves caressed the Reef. She tried thinking about other things, Hatteras, her teaching job—could she go back to any of that? She knew Laurel Nash surely would have been listed as 'lost at sea'. Just as her father's ship would've.... She despised Mathropos for dredging up that memory—and not just in a fleeting, oh yeah this happened kind of way. Full on hardcore 4K emotion as if she were living through Dad's death moment by moment as she had the first time.

Damn Fates.

But the fresh tears rolling down her cheeks did not fall for her father. Being aboard Trutina's vessel reminded her of being aboard Dad's ship: *The Ghost.* How many decks had she walked with her father in her lifetime? Since being rescued by Trutina over a year ago, she'd not journeyed on water since and it *felt* like she'd not been on a ship since *The Ghost* had gone down.   Laurel wanted someone to say it could have happened to anyone, even a seasoned sailor—but the truth was she had lost the one thing in the whole world Dad had loved as much as Laurel...as much as her mother. But no one could grant her such a reprieve. Not even Paul.

The night she'd shared the sinking with him, he seemed unnaturally captivated by the where and the how of the sinking. She had cried herself to sleep in his arms, listening to him saying, *Nothing is ever lost at sea Laurie...Thalassa knows where she keeps all her treasures.*

Thalassa, he'd called the ocean and she should have questioned him then but she just filed it under his vernacular. She knew if she combed through all their conversations she'd find other clues.

She missed him. The sound of her special name in his mouth with that resonant lilt only Greeks can manifest always gave her new buoyancy. Except Paul wasn't exactly just a Greek. He was more. The thought exhilarated and frightened her. As she considered it more deeply, it actually kind of pissed her off that he would hide it from her for so long.

"Do these agree with you?" Trutina held out a pair of beige linen capris and a coral linen camp shirt.

"Oh shit!   You startled me; I didn't even hear you approach." She scanned his face but discerned no measurable amount of emotion, recognition...life.

"Ay-yuh. Can you wear this attire?" Still no expression, his white eyes barely blinked.

"Thank you." She took them. Trutina shifted slightly, perhaps to stare out at the Reef. "You *are* blind, right?"

His thin smile surprised her. "The ocean is my eyes. You may don your clothing here; we are leagues from those who see by other means." Still, perhaps out of courtesy, he turned his back to her.

She pulled the filthy shift off over her head, pondering only briefly the whereabouts of the elegant chiton Paul had laid out for her forever ago. Beneath the shift, her naked body welcomed the fading rays of the sun, adding just the right brilliance to her bronzed skin. Her stomach had tightened over the last several months and her arms had picked up the tone she'd promised herself many times before to work on. As she slid into the capri's, she worried they'd be too small, but again time with Paul had reduced and tightened her thighs as well.

Laurel wadded up the shift and poured what remained in the decanter into it, using it to wash her face and under her arms and breasts. As she finished, the world around her seemed to breathe with new vigor: several flocks of Piping Plover and Laughing gulls scavenged alongside a few Caspian tern; the sun had all but vanished below the horizon. The constant whisper of the ocean waves and the warm air seemed a lullaby in tandem with the gentle rocking of the ship. Shimmery cirrus clouds displayed a vibrant gold and red mural in the wake of the setting sun. "If my father were standing here with me, he'd say *Red sky at night, sailor's delight...red sky in the morn—sailor be warned.*" She laughed a small laugh, slightly embarrassed to have shared the memory with Trutina. Of everything else, Laurel had no idea what her father would say.

Trutina remained tacit, his back to her still.

She dropped the shift and slipped into the camp shirt, grateful she still wore a bra because the shirt fit a little too tightly around the chest. Her shoulder and hip hurt, probably from being tossed aboard by Ulgos. A vague headache hovered at her left temple. She watched Trutina for a moment longer, admiring the fine muscles in his back and arms, and how his hairless head reflected the waning sunlight. Her recollection of Greek mythology did not include him but she wasn't sure how the citizens of Olympos would react to such questions. She decided to hold her questions for another time. "I'm finished. And thank you for being a gentleman."

"He speaks truth; you are beautiful." Trutina skiff-skaffed to the stern, checking the sails, ballast, and all the rigging as he went—each with a mere touch of his fingers.

"Who speaks truth? Is there someone else onboard?" Laurel looked aft and stern, stepping closer to the center mast, then moving forward enough to peer around the cabin doors, and below deck. She saw eight steps leading down into darkness but heard nothing that indicated additional passengers.

"Your Paul," Trutina called from behind her; he hung from the rigging of the mizzen, clambering diagonally down and across the netting with the ease and grace of a spider-monkey.

"My Paul. But you know him as Poseidon." She watched his fluid dance across the rigging, marveling at his prowess despite being blind.

"Ay-yuh. I and he know each other well." He never faltered or paused in his ministrations to the sails and rigging.

"Trutina, you said that we met here, at the...what did you call it: Afay-oss?"

"Yfalos," he corrected.

"Eee-fahl-ose...Yfalos. The Reef. Is this how I would get back home? Back to Hatteras, ah, I mean Earthside? If I jumped overboard now and swam to the Reef and shouted

Clattu, Verrata, Nicktu would I be plopped in the middle of Crete? Zante? Maybe Lefkada...that's kind of a bit north in the Ionian Sea. Can I jump out of an ancient oracle in Athens?"

Trutina never responded. He maneuvered about the ketch with greater agility than a sighted man.

"Not a big chatter box are you?" Nothing. "If we're going to Athena's island then—"

"We sail already." He appeared beside her silently.

"Oh my God, *please* stop doing that." She collected herself and continued. "I'm impressed—my father, he knew ships very well but you? I've never seen anyone better with a ship than my father."

The forty-foot ketch moved steadily away from the Yfalos, The Reef—to the east Laurel thought. Overhead, a few dozen sapphires gleamed in the darkening sky. "I didn't even see you weigh anchor; let alone feel it." She frowned and resigned herself to the fact that it would be longer than she expected before she had her sea-legs again. *Listen to your bones, lil'fin.* I wish I could, Dad.

Trutina swayed gently from side to side in rhythm with the ketch's waltz upon the waves. He did not offer any comment or ask for explanations.

For a moment she found herself feeling at ease, as if they sailed idly across the Atlantic instead of Olympian waters. The moment drifted away from her as she caught the owl's head pendant with her hand. Faintly, at a distance impossible to measure but far enough away to feel like forever, she sensed Paul.

"He said you would not remember. I am unaccustomed to your...idiosyncrasies. Time blurs for one such as I. When last I ferried one such as you, twas afore the war." Trutina brushed past her to the mizzen where he made adjustments, increasing their speed ever so slightly. The wind against her face felt rejuvenating, the air fresh and rich in a peculiar way. She touched her internal GPS, that sense of direction she had inherited from her father,—Dad called it his human compass—but right now, for Laurel, it spun aimlessly. *Enough time and distance....* She hoped Paul was right. "I used to be able to judge direction by the wind, sun...the stars —I don't know where we are now. My compass is...broken, I guess." She soaked in the buffeting winds.

"Should you know?" He asked matter-of-factly.

"My Dad raised me on the water, practically—he served twenty-seven years in the U.S. Coast Guard. After that it was eleven years of listening to him talk endlessly about *The Voyage.*

"Gonna take *Ghost* all the way to Greece, lil'fin he'd say. He wanted to see the home of democracy and...I think he wanted to do it for Mom. After he died, I took The Voyage for him. It sounds so simple now..." she looked at the old seaman trying to decipher the weathered skin surrounding the milky white eyes. "Let's just say I thought I knew a lot about the sea and found out the hard way, I didn't." Anger suddenly roiled up from within her. She said quickly, "Where are we? How far away from Athena's island are we?" A hot spear of hatred pulsed from temple to temple followed by a watery image of Paul and two men arguing then the visage dissolved into colored droplets. As it dissipated, she felt Paul drifting further away, the hatred lingering.

Trutina proceeded to light five lanterns suspended from nails in the mizzen and center mast as well as two smaller globe-shaped lanterns flanking the cabin doorway. The amber glow of the lights made the deck of the ship young again. Laurel's attention was drawn once more to the mural on the deck. The once stationary figures now seemed animated in the flickering shadows, clashing together silently within the grain of the aged deck.

"This is a beautiful mural," she moved closer, the hatred fading. Among the combatants depicted, she could see smaller figures cowering beneath whorls of flame sweeping just over their heads. To the left and right of the faded central figure she found a pair of majestic black stallions. Beside or behind the steed on the left she saw three women dressed in gray robes that might once have been blue. Two of the women stood immediately behind the third; all three of them were watching the battle with absent expressions. Laurel squatted to get a closer look, and could see that the two women in the background had their hands on the shoulders of the third woman. Between their out stretched hands, laced through their splayed fingers, a mosaic of knot-choked threads dangled.

"Damn Fates," she muttered; her fingers floated over their likenesses. "Is this him?" she asked hesitantly. *You can do this; it's okay to know him as Poseidon.* It wasn't the same as finding out Paul was an adulterer or an ex-con. Still, those things made sense to her and although they showed up in fiction—they were also very real. Poseidon, Olympos, the damn Fates—all that originated in Homer and Plato and all those ancient Greek fellows. "I can't really make it out but I'm guess this is Paul...Poseidon."

"It is better that way." Trutina remarked.

"How is it better? Listen, I'm not a ten year old who just found out that Santa isn't real. You can be honest with me." She toyed with the pendant, drawing only a sliver of comfort.

"They and Poseidon battle for the Reef. He won. But at a great price." He appeared to be looking directly at her, his face a flickering mask of shadows. The lanterns gave his eyes an unnatural glow. He almost appeared sighted.

"How long ago was this?" she swallowed back more questions. *Is he like the Poseidon I know from the* Iliad *or the* Odyssey? She did not think Trutina would know those. There were other, more dangerous questions. Old Poppa had said that Trutina's debt to Poseidon was greater than any other upon Olympos. It was too early to play that trump card.

"We shall reach Athena's island by tomorrow, if Aeolus allows."

"I don't like it when you do that. Answer one of my questions from twenty-minutes ago but ignore the present question."

"What has been set in motion cannot be stopped." He moved only to make minor adjustments of the helm.

Laurel felt her ire rising again. She watched the waters, examined the unknown constellations overhead but none of them provided a distraction from her wayward emotions. "I'm hoping you can—"

"How much time do you have?"

"...help me with...what do you mean?"

"Poseidon did not set off on this quest with the luxury of laxity."

"Trutina, I know you said that you haven't dealt with an Earthsider in some time but I'm getting the impression that you haven't dealt with *anyone* in some time. I don't know what you mean about time."

"Ay-yuh."

"Ok, that's getting a little annoying." She felt hot, red faced hot. She wanted to break something. "So, so, what? I'm just supposed to buy every cryptic line of bullshit you dish out because you're a wise old blind seafaring fella? Let me guess, you're my guide who intermittently but surreptitiously provides clues to my present dilemma; like some kind of literary archetype? What happens now, you calm me down and explain to me that everything's going to be ok? And *do not* say ay-yuh!"

Trutina tilted his head to the left, listening.

"Fine. If you won't talk about him, then what about them? The Fates? Mira, Makaisi and that she-bitch Mathropos." She stomped her foot on the image of the center woman repeatedly; it had to be Mathropos. She willed it to be Mathropos. The slamming of her foot against the deck felt good. She continued. "Where I come from, they're decrepit old hags almost as enigmatic as you, old sea faring fella." She laughed, darkly.

Laurel heard herself but couldn't stop. She took up the pendant but it did nothing to delineate the deluge of rage building in her system. Words erupted from her unrestrained. Words and truths she wasn't prepared to spill before a stranger: "Well let me just lay out something for you. I screwed up. I abandoned *everything* and left North Carolina on my father's leaky, shitty, run down boat and then, *then* I sank the damn thing. That's right, it sank and then you hauled my ass outta the water and dropped me off on Paul's island...*Ha!* Poseidon's Isle, and I fell in love with him. And then do you know what? Yep, you guessed the pattern: Lost my dad, lost his ship, and then I *lost Paul!*" she was screaming her words, spit and tears flew from her face.

Trutina had yet to turn or even acknowledge her.

"This *hurts!*" she wailed helplessly, feeling trapped in her own head listening at a distance but feeling everything up close and personal.   "*AAAAAGGGGGHHHH!*" she bellowed a wail out across the ocean and fell to her knees.

"We are distant from their charms, now." Trutina stood

beside her, his voice subdued. "No, do not stand yet—there is more to come for you." he knelt beside her and gingerly pulled sweat soaked black curls away from her face.

"Wh-what do you mean? More?" as she said it the rage inside reached critical mass and burned behind her heart. Everything the Fates had done to her, every moment of self-loathing she'd tried to drink away after her father's death, every ounce of guilt she harbored over losing *The Ghost* all fused into one single infinite scream.

"This too shall pass." He whispered to her softly.

She felt the dark hate leave her abruptly without any fanfare or residue. She looked at the Angler wondering what he saw of her with his ocean-site. She looked away, ashamed.

"I am sorry, Isa—" he stopped, closed his eyes and swallowed the rest of the name. "I am sorry, Earthsider." He did not leave her.

"It's ok. I'm sorry I yelled at you." She remembered something, a moment locked by the Fates perhaps—maybe it wasn't even real. She felt compelled to say it and quickly in case she forgot it all again. "I remember smelling the sheets where Paul died." A cry fell from her lips, but she continued. "I...I couldn't find him. I don't even know if this really h-happened or they made it be a memory or...I don't know. I just remember not knowing where he was and I thought he was playing a trick on me...And then I remembered he died."

Trutina kissed her forehead and she heard him whisper *I'm sorry Isa* again.

Before she could ask what he meant, deep weariness fell upon her with the same intensity as the previous rage.

"Time and distance," Trutina said, cradling her in his arms. He rocked her in motion with the dance of the ship until her eyes fluttered shut for a time.

TWELVE

Amynta wanted to trust the boy, Icarus. But time and distance had done little to erase the damage his father had caused during the war. She read Daedulus in the boy's face, the hard lines lurking beneath the youthful vigor; the mischievous glint poised to become a diabolical flare.

"So, that was just a little weird don't you think?" he paced around the anteroom of Poseidon's inner sanctum, his wings twitching now and then.

It would be easy to underestimate him. "Aye, The Keeper seemed...beleaguered. Another matter another time, boy. What have you come here for and why?" Amynta leveled her motherly glare upon him.

"For a pencil...pensive...*purpose!* Aye, for a purpose I am bound not to share—"

Amynta moved closer to him, her nose an inch from his face. "By whose oath?"

Icarus backpedaled, stumbling against the wall. "Lord Poseidon's." the lack of color in his face confirmed the truth.

Amynta adjusted her robes, maintaining her glare a moment longer before ending the boy's torment. "You are free to tell me. I am Lord Poseidon's oikonomos; he entrusted me with the keeping of the Lighthouse so if there is anything here which you must retrieve then I—"

"I am bound, Amynta. I cannot discuss my mission with anyone." The hard lines surfaced briefly.

"What is your father up to, boy?" she would have to tread carefully. Seeing Makaisi likely set the boy's hackles on fire in much the same way hers would be if Daedulus had come in Icarus' stead.

"Oh well he loves gardening and reading...I haven't seen him doing much tinkering lately but that's surely on the list." His wide smile softened the lines.

Amynta resisted echoing his smile. *Time and distance* she found herself repeating. "Olympos surely changes this day," she muttered and left the boy to his grin. She unlocked Poseidon's *sanctum-sanctorum* and entered her master's inner chambers without a second thought. She tidied the bed he and the Earthsider had shared for nearly a year, a task which she'd not had to perform in an age or two. It did cross her mind while she tucked corners and fluffed pillows that except for the Earthsider, Lord Poseidon had had no other lovers in the Lighthouse.

"Or at all, I suppose." She muttered aloud.

"I'm sorry, did you say *Geritol*? I don't see how that's going to help. Not in the least; for that matter I suspect finding such an Earthsider remedy upon the island would be next to impossible."

Amynta had forgotten about the boy. She tightened her glare and resolved to complete what she'd set out to do regardless of any further interruptions. "If you are here to spy for your father, it would be best for you to leave."

"If you believe what you hear about my father it would be best for *you* to reconsider the source." His voice faltered only once and she was certain if she gazed upon him now his face would be an exact, if not younger, replica of Daedulus.

"Boy, I do not have the time—"

"Neither do I, Amynta. I recognize your authority here, but mark me—I did not come to parlay—I am here at Lord Poseidon's request. The who, what, where, when, why, and how of which need not be any of your concern."

Perhaps, Amynta mused, Icarus would be a better man than his father. "Be about it then, boy. I have matters to attend to as well." She crossed her arms beneath her breasts and waited.

Icarus fidgeted, his wings flexing out then in. "I cannot... not with you here. I am sorry." The boyishness melted her. But she could not be at ease around him as much as she wished to show him compassion—it was not his fault his father had caused the death of her husband.

"So be it, boy. I will return to the Lighthouse in ten minutes time. If you are finished by then you ought be gone; if you are not then best you move more swiftly."

Icarus bowed to her. "I will make hassle... waste?...*Haste!*" He turned away from her, stopped and then brought wide deep blue eyes to hers. "Amynta. I am sorry you have suffered. I will tell you this: he hurts more than you will ever be able to measure." He nodded, assured that he'd said what needed saying.

Amynta said nothing as she left Icarus alone in the Lighthouse, but her thoughts returned to believing. "Time and distance," she spoke the mantra gently.

THIRTEEN

Icarus did not wait for Amynta to return.

He secured what he'd been sent to retrieve and leapt from the crown of the Lighthouse flying hard and fast, his wings snapping against the air with a satisfying *quaffack!*

Fly to her, bring her this gift, do not *fail me.* Even now, Poseidon's words still sent an electric resonance coruscating down Icarus' spine. *A lifetime had passed since Poseidon had asked Da for help but no god had ever come to me first! So this is how it begins! This is the adventure, the hero's quest, the epic journey!*

The boy smiled widely then dropped the grin quickly fearful of moths, feathers, and other unpleasant objects he had had to remove from his teeth more than once. He swooped up, hung briefly on a thermal, and then descended in a wide diagonal arc toward the surface of the sea.

Fly to her, he repeated Lord Poseidon's words over and over in his head.

Fly to *her*.

Fly *to her*.

Icarus thrust his wings back, pulling deep for greater speed.

This could be our time, Da.

He hoped. He strained for more hope. Icarus had taken the burden of indebtedness without consulting his father so there would be no turning back now. All he had to do was reach the Earthsider before she reached Athena.

The Earthsider.

He had heard the stories but he had yet to meet her. Meeting her would be as close to going Earthside as he could imagine. The anticipation burned him to his wing tips.

He had to push the wings, push them past any expectations, calculations, or limitations his father had ever considered. And since his father just happened to be the Master Inventor for the Gods of Olympos that meant Icarus had no room for error.

Well, there was always hedgeroom, even with Da's mechanical marvels and impossible inventions.

Faster then, he willed himself.

He *would* undo what had been done. He *would* pay his father's debt to Poseidon.

Even if that means confronting The Judge again, once and for all.

He flew on toward the Earthsider.

FOURTEEN

Mathropos extracted twelve threads from the dying man.

She swirled them in her mouth relishing the flavor of a life lived without success. His name slipped across her thoughts like a discarded oyster: Deidros Papadopoulos. Salty patches revealed a history of his shortcomings and disillusionment with the gods.

Deidros stared into Mathropos, the life he'd squandered on false hopes and unfulfilled prophecies drizzled out of him in much the same manner milk can be purged from a goat's teat.

She did not wait for his final breath, extracting the last few threads as she dropped the husk of his body onto the skiff she'd pulled him from.

The seizures fell upon her almost immediately, this time, contorting her frame as if Zeus himself had entered her bones and sought to rework them into some new creature. Her skin undulated head to toe, back to front as the new threads assimilated themselves with the others. Mathropos' right eye bulged and then settled into a fixed glazed-over stare while the left eye darted back and forth in protest to this torture.

But I am The Keeper.

And she willed her body to behave itself; there was work to be done and she had no time for such disruptions.

Still, it took another fourteen seconds before she felt completely in control. A worry she would have to address with Fa—

"Sister, where have you been?" Makaisi stepped from a fold in the air.

Mathropos regarded the water lapping at the shoreline of Athena's island and found that it reminded her of the futility of the Earthsider's quest. Fate is like the water: mercurial, elusive, and can take the shape of any vessel into which it is poured. Over time or all at once, Fate can be a destructive force against which nothing can long stand whole. "I had matters to attend to, *sister*. Where is Mira?"

Makaisi nodded absently, her look scrutinizing. "She is but a moment behind. What were you—"

"Choose your accusations with care, Makaisi. My tolerance for your insubordination is not what it once was." Mathropos nudged the skiff away from the shoreline with enough force to send it into the surf. The man and his vessel were consumed after the second wave. A marvelous thing, Fate.

Makaisi wisely chose to say nothing, walking beside Mathropos in silence as they strolled along the beach.

"You are certain the Threads of the Earthsider, the boy, and the Angler are bound?" Mathropos asked even though she could read the answer herself.

"Aye. Although...No. 'Tis nothing. Ahh, here is Mira now." Makaisi smirked as she waved to their hefty sister.

"Do not toy with me, Makaisi. Your distractions carry no weight." Mathropos did not take her eyes off Makaisi. Contempt ebbed along the Threads but something else writhed beneath. She could not extract the feeling to identify it, and this troubled her deeply. *You carry so much—too much—I know but it will all be worth it. Soon.*

"Sisters! You must hurry." Mira's size did not prevent her from reaching them in short order.

Makaisi's mouth held its slight sneer.

"I hope it is not another senseless struggle with Poseidon; as I have told you countless times already: Keep him suspended *above* the water—"

"It pertains to the *Dunamis*, Mathropos. It is gone." Mira, out of breath and drenched in sweat, had only set foot in the shadow of her sisters' before Mathropos moved all three of them along the Threads toward Anaktoro.

What trickery could this be? None but the Fates and the brother-gods knew of the existence of the *Dunamis*. And only she and Poseidon knew of its precise location. What catastrophe had the ocean-god concocted now? The time to lay the final Weave and end this game had finally arrived. *I shall hurt the gods as they have never been pained before! And for their own good, for the good of Olympos this must be done.*

She would have to consume more threads in order to manipulate the Master Weave but when she was finished all would be as it had been. And the gods would once and for all be able to reclaim their rightful place as rulers of the Earth-siders; while she alone would become Fate over them all.

Not simply influence it, or measure or cut it, but I *shall be Fate itself! If Father wills it to be so....*

Mathropos moved them along the Threads with all the speed she could muster, suppressing her fears over her deteriorating control. She needed but consume more threads and all would be as it should have been from the beginning.

FIFTEEN

Poseidon loves me.

Laurel traced the owl's head pendant with the pinky of her left hand as she watched Trutina steer the old ketch through the darkness of this mythical ocean. She had lost one day to fatigue and strife. Because of the Fates.

Because of losing Paul.

The pendant remained empty and silent. For now at least, the absence was tolerable. Presently, her thoughts remained fixed on her breakdown. Why the sudden rage? What caused it: Paul, Poseidon, or the Fates? She considered briefly that it was simply her fatigued brain battling the reality of her situation. Her bones told her it was something more, so she'd been dwelling on what exactly that might be when she recalled Trutina's peculiar behavior. She worked the pendant fervently, aching for a clue...a whisper.

He called me Isa. *I know he did. I heard it. He's keeping something from me, I can feel it.* She didn't need a magic pendant or the love of a god to confirm that truth. Still, as enigmatic as Trutina was, he was entitled to keep secrets from an Earthsider. *Really, Laurel do you think that just because Poseidon's you're lover that suddenly you're entitled to know* everything *that's going on?* It was true: She had no say over this world, Poseidon's lover or not and there was nothing to be gained in trying to figure out a man like Trutina when greater things weighed on her shoulders. Nonetheless, the fact remained that although he called her Isa, it was really more of how he coddled her that left such an imprint.

Whoever Isa was to Trutina, she certainly was lost to him and that brought Laurel skirting along the curious parallel to her own situation, fearful that Paul had somehow bound her to Trutina in a way she might regret.

There's no sense to be made of what a rock's thinkin' lil'fin. Better to work with it than against it—at least then your work's getting' done. Her father, unfortunately, rarely made time for the rocks that needed the most work. Like his daughter. She took up the pendant again, accepting that she would not solve the mystery of Trutina in one day. Laurel knew she'd have to wait this one out, let the solution come to her. That was how she'd have to deal with being in love with Poseidon.

The god of oceans both Earthside and upon Olympos has given me his heart. Laurel took a long, deep breath of salt air, working the owl's head pendant between her fingers. She wanted him again, wanted to feel his hands on her body, in her hair—she wanted to taste his skin and be kissed in all the places only Paul knew.

Trutina hummed and sang as he guided *The Balance* through the night, the words and music spectral, alluring. The Grecian words crackled with depth and meaning she sensed would only be understood by the gods. Yet, the song resonated in her bones, soothing her. For a time she simply watched the rolling dark waters and thought of nothing else.

She looked out across the ocean where the light of the

moon painted silver streaks over the still, oil-black canvas. *Who will I find at the end of this journey, Paul or Poseidon? Man or god?* "No sense to be made of what a rock is thinking, right Dad?"

Laurel stopped playing with the pendant and stepped back from the railing, finally feeling her sea legs smoothly take control. Sailing on the ketch did not make her nostalgic, if anything it resurrected buried pains. Since losing Dad's ship, *The Ghost*, she had not been out to sea—not even at Paul's insistence.

I did not mean to wake your ire, Laurie...I thought you were a woman of the sea. I know that your father—

He's dead, Paul and I can't. I failed him.

You navigated your way here, did you not?

Laurel paced to the port side railing, weaving her way through coils of rope, two thick bellied barrels, and an impressive collection of fishing tackle, rods, and netting.

The ketch did remind her of one she'd toured with Dad what seemed a hundred years ago. It had been her twenty-first birthday and a profound moment in the Nash household: Bill Koch brought the America's Cup back home with the crew of the *America 3* that year, and Nathan Nash was by God going to give his daughter one hella-grand birthday! Although they could not attend the race, she and Dad drove south along the Outer Banks, stayed a weekend in Ocracoke —they even filled out an application to race in the 28th annual Indian Island to Ocracoke Regatta; though they never did get to race that one. She smiled widely, remembering how alive Dad had been, how much fun they'd had together —it was one of the last times she was able to completely and totally forget about pursuing her degree in Wilmington and focus entirely on Dad.

She leaned heavily on the rail, spray from the prow

lightly misting her face. Fifteen feet shorter and considerably older, Trutina's ship did not share much with the *Christiana*. She was a 45-footer so rich with brightwork it seemed covered in silver and brass neon lighting. Her glossy fiberglass hull was a ruse, Dad had explained. *There's a wooden skeleton in that closet, Lil'fin—she won't see too many more floatplans.* Dad loved being the boat guy. At every regatta, every yacht club, every port, he made everyone aware of this limitless knowledge about ships from canoes to ketchs to a jack-ass barque. Even now, as she looked up at the square-rigged main and mizzen masts she knew her father would gladly have engaged Trutina in a discussion about the thirty degree difference of course between this ship and a tri-mast ship with fore and aft sail rigging.

What am I supposed to do, Dad? She forced the thought to travel to the heavens where she held to the notion that Nathan Nash, though incorporeal, existed in some form. It had to be possible—Poseidon had been her lover after all. But if the thought reached her father, it was a one way street. She listened to the waters instead, remembering her father at various times. Little pockets of memories like icons on an iPhone *plipped* into her thoughts.

Touch one and *plip!* and it showed him young and sharply dressed in his Coastie Alphas. Touch another *plip* and there's Dad jumping up and down on a trampoline at the Wilmington County Fair.

Plip! Dad racing her with a Wal-mart shopping cart and crashing into an endcap of papertowels.

Plip! and Dad's scolding her for staying with Mark for so long, his words popping out of his mouth like an animated advertisement on a website: *He's not good for you...He's lazy... arrogant...he's cheated on you* how *many times?*

Plip! There he is sad and gray standing over Mom's grave.

She held that one longer, watching him tell the headstone he missed her without saying a word. They visited her grave every year on December 1st. Not a birthday, not a death-day, not even their wedding day. It was the day she told him no...*No Nathaniel Bowditch Nash*: *I will not marry you.* And she didn't. For an entire year Dad courted her in the way a proper southern gentleman should. Laurel replayed the memory twice more, listening to her father's dry leaf-rasp cinch up as he remembered Mrs. Evie Nash.

Laurel pulled out of her reverie to the darkness around her, cut only mildly by the curious orb lanterns suspended from the panels outside the hatch doors. Their yellow-green glow did not penetrate beyond the outhaul overhead, but kept the companionway adequately lit just the same. A few feet up the starboard gangway, tucked between the mizzen and main masts and curiously higher than most pilothouses, Trutina stood alone, stoic, perhaps sibylline? He seemed capable and willing to answer direct questions but then only on his time and even then quite succinctly.

When pressed about the Fates or their ability to reach them all Trutina could say was, "We remain within their touch."

She thought about the sisters and their damn Threads; about Paul's funeral and if it meant anything at all. She thought about the last year with Paul...and if *that* meant anything at all. How could she not have known he was Poseidon? Or that she wasn't Earthside? How did he keep all that from her? She knew the answer; it had little to do with Paul and almost everything to do with her.

Taking a deep, shaking breath, Laurel walked up to the pilothouse and stood just to the right of Trutina. She watched the ocean before them, silvery and black beneath the moon's illumination. She gauged their speed to be somewhere between 15 and 20 knots. With the wind twisting through her curls, she felt oddly relieved to be moving, headed toward something. "Do you mind some company?" she tried to keep her voice even and failed miserably.

"You changed him." Trutina sang.

"What?"

"Being with him, you changed him. You changed you." he did not take his gaze off the wine dark waters" ahead.

"Did I? And how would you know? I mean, I get that you 'know' him. Poseidon. You have no idea how weird it is for me to say that out loud. Do you? I don't know, I can't tell by your blank expression. How did I change a...a...*god*?!"

The resentment she tried to mask drew Trutina's pupil-less eyes to hers. "There is a bunk for you below." His expression remained impassive but his voice belied a current of bitterness.

"We remain within their touch, hm? Is that what you're thinking? Because I am. I'm thinking that all of this is too much. You treat me like I'm supposed to know more, like I get all of this. Well I don't. And I'd appreciate a little more compassion."

"You did not change the god. You changed the man." Trutina returned his gaze to the ocean.

She started to say she was sorry, even raised her hand to squeeze his shoulder but stopped. Because he knew. Like her father knew. She trembled, realizing how eerily similar the two men behaved. *I'm Dorothy in Oz and I'm going to wake up to tell all my friends what a crazy-ass dream I had about the Olympians. So where are my fuckin ruby slippers then?*

Except the sway of the ship beneath her feet felt natural, integral to her being. The smell of the salt, of the water-worn wood...the scent of this sun-soaked man....

"I...will..see you tomorrow, Trutina. Thank you." She left him, afraid to look back and see those panoptic whites peeling away her defenses. Just like Dad would do. She felt leveled, suddenly, and then compelled to offer a final word: "Trutina, may the winds of Aeolus favor you again." Laurel hurried away, her brain shuddering from being hijacked —*Where the hell did that come from?*—but she knew as soon as she thought it. In fact she could smell him now, faintly and fleeting but it was him and she smiled.

Paul.

Laurel held on to his presence for as long as she could, but like mercury in her palm it split and evaded every attempt to contain it. Even holding the pendant against her chest could not stay his essence. But it was enough to go on, enough to excite her, enough for now.

She made her way below decks, finding the narrow hallway lit by a trio of smaller glow-orbs. Of the three doors, each richly stained in a glossy cherry, the last was the only one unlocked. Inside, she found a sparsely decorated room not much larger than a closet. To the right stood a squat, fat chest of drawers which seemed an extension of the dark paneled wall. Atop the dresser, Trutina had laid a pair of green plaid sleep pants and matching shirt, a brush, a stand mirror, a set of wash cloths, and above all of this he had hung a small glow-orb. To her left rested an ornate porcelain wash basin atop a dark oak pedestal which had been bolted to the floor. A ring of cobalt blue owls flew eternally around the rim of the basin. Opposite the door stood the uninviting bunk. Again, the dark paneling which surrounded the room also embraced the face of the bunk; however, rather than the mundane parallel lines of the paneling, this piece boasted a pair of peacocks staring at one another over what appeared to be ivy.

Laurel ran her hands over the turned down blankets and back up under the round pillow. She had not slept alone since, well, since Paul's death. If you could call that sleeping. Funny how she hadn't thought about it until now, not sleeping beside him, feeling his chest move in different rhythms as he fell into deeper sleep. She thought of the speckled black and white forest of hair on his chest, the tautness of his belly, how the smell of his skin always reminded her of sea air and water-wood.

She changed into the sleep pants and shirt quickly, and then washed her face and neck with the water in the owl basin. Afterward, she slipped into the bunk and pulled the covers up to her chin. Her fingers toyed with the owl's head pendant.

What now?

How will sleep come?

When will we be far enough away so that I can know absolutely that my thoughts and memories are my own?

When sleep finally did come, it was as a thief, stealing her thoughts, questions, worries and dreams...at least momentarily.

SIXTEEN

Trutina's hands remained fused with the grain of the wood of the helm long after the Earthsider left him. To extract them would double the pain he endured simply having her aboard *The Balance.*

Such is the cost of a blood debt. Every word from her mouth a lashing, every footstep on the deck a branding.

Off the port side bow, half a league at best, the shimmering air alerted him to the approaching visitor. He had expected this. From the moment Poseidon broke his own laws to board *The Balance,* Trutina knew this would be his penance. He guided the ketch without moving his hands or the helm, no need for such trivialities with the Earthsider belowdecks. The woodgrain gradually released his skin, the deeper burning, however, would never diminish while she remained aboard.

As he neared the shimmering air, he wondered if she knew how deeply into the grain of her wood her skin had become fused. To have the love of a god was one matter; to have him risk the lives of every denizen of Olympos for you was something else entirely.

"*How does it feel to be a ferryman again?*" the visitor asked in a thrumming timbre that resonated through the deckwood of *The Balance*.

Trutina chose not to respond. He tended to the rigging, listening, waiting.

"*Your brother sends his well-wishes; he's a bit more conversational than you. That's saying a good deal considering Charon has no tongue.*" The visitor chuckled at his jest.

The ship cut the ocean surface seamlessly, creating a whisper of a wake and moving so quickly that an observer likely would see only a blur of her form. And though he would never speak such, he was invigorated to be a ferryman again.

"I came to thank you, Angler." the visitor confided unexpectedly, his voice leveling into normal speech patterns though no less harmonious.

Trutina nearly stumbled as he descended the mizzen's rigging. He lighted upon the deck with ease, though, standing to face the aurulent visage of the visitor.

"You know he cannot do so himself. Nor can the other until this puzzle is complete. Or the whole of it is broken. You carry this debt, Angler, with more honor than I have seen in men carrying debts half so weighty." The visitor paused and his presence seemed to lose power, a harsh breeze threatening to douse a mighty fire. This spoke volumes of the effort required simply to be here, let alone to travel in tandem with a swift-moving ship.

"I do not wish for your pains to go without reward so I have arranged a...moment. For you." The visitor's golden hues stuttered briefly, then shifted to a thin silver and finally a smoky ochre out of which emanated *her* song.

"Isa..." he breathed out her name. He did not move for fear it would disrupt the illusion.

"As agreed, Angler, your suffering shall be rewarded...in time...all debts forgiven." The visitor's voice shook with the effort to maintain the moment.

Trutina held himself in check, the effort would have impressed Herakles himself. For a minute he even forgot the pain of escorting the Earthsider. And then the visitor could no longer maintain the moment. Even as the ochre window imploded back to silver, then a weaker gold than before, Isa's song clung to him, fused itself into the grain of his soul. Trutina closed his eyes and saw her, the true compass of *The Balance*. He smiled despite himself.

"*I cannot do this again, Trutina.*" The visitor's voice swiftly resumed its volcanic rumbling resonance. "*You understand the risk. Know that you are not alone in your suffering. We do this for all of us...for all of them.*"

Trutina bowed. He did understand. The visitor indeed had risked a great deal just being here, let alone granting him the luxury of Isa's lost song. And he understood something new, something he had always taken for granted but had never before now actually experienced: the love of the gods for their subjects.

The shimmering air shook violently and Trutina knew their meeting was at an end. He lifted his head to face the visitor and a smile spread through the sun soaked creases of his face. He spoke with revitalized conviction, with a belief in the truth of words he'd simply grown accustomed to saying for the sake of saying them: *time and distance*. He cleared his throat and took hold of the helm again, the grain pulling his skin snugly into the wooden torture. "I shall protect the Earthsider and see her to her destination without harm. On this you have my blood oath."

As the image faded, gold flecks winked out like violently

extinguished fireflies and the visitor spoke a final time: "*Fare thee well, Trutina.*"

"Fare thee well...Lord Hades."

SEVENTEEN

Amynta stood over Oli and Harlan as they slept. The night had not come quickly enough and now the dawn lay only hours away.

And she had not slept a moment for fear that the sisters would make good their threat of harm upon her sons.

Poseidon's island had finally settled, her waters, weather, and people torn by the changes could not be mended in an evening. They may never be mended, truth be told. She stepped over to the boys' window and watched the moonlight embrace each wave as it crested and fell upon the shore. She measured the rhythm but did not take much relief in the familiarity. This too will change, she knew. The god of the seas and oceans cannot die without consequence to his charges. But she knew that before any of this started. Before the war.

Before the Earthsider's arrival what seemed a decade ago.

Even the boys had asked about Laurel today.

Amynta lied to them, allowing them to believe the Earthsider had gone to join Poseidon in his chambers upon Anaktoro, Zeus' home. That they missed her took some of the burden off Amynta's heart for involving them in the first place. It was bad enough their father had had to prove himself and die doing so, she did not care to fill their heads with more adventure. She had to keep them safe as long as possible.

Until this conflict ended.

Until Olympos was whole or *everything* was no more.

She pulled away from the window and returned to the table upon which she had laid what Lord Poseidon had charged her with safekeeping. As innocent in appearance as Oli or Harlan, the figurine hardly seemed worth the trouble she'd gone to in retrieving it. But she knew its meaning. She knew the truth and though keeping it meant certain peril for her, she also knew without it her boys would never be safe.

Amynta lifted the galloping horse and marveled at its detail. "Your kin may be distant from you but we shall see you reunited soon." She admired her master's cleverness, for a man, at least. Still, the Fates had their own cleverness and if they knew she held a third of her master's might in her hands there would be no laws left unbroken in their lust to possess it.

For now, it remained an intricate pewter casting of a horse galloping through waves. If the Earthsider succeeded in reaching Athena's island and beyond then two-thirds of the trident would be closer to its master.

Keep this for me, Amynta. If I fail—

But you cannot!

If I fail then from Hades you must seek protection. This *shall pay your passage.*

She watched Oli and Harlan sleeping, hoping that their dreams were their own and not tainted by residual reso-nances left by the Fates. Amynta did not know what she would do if the time came for her to stand against the sisters, let alone the other gods who opposed Lord Poseidon and the brother gods. But she knew what needed doing now and that would carry her to the next that needed doing. It would, in the end, be no different than cleaning up the messy room of a child.

Her hands slipped into her apron pockets where she retrieved a length of hemp. Deftly, she wound the figurine's neck and hind quarters until it was satisfactorily bound. After a moment she had fashioned the galloping horse into a somewhat cumbersome but otherwise elegant bracelet. Amynta slipped it over her left wrist, tested the weight and decided it would take some getting used to before she could ignore it altogether.

Looking at the horse in the moonlight slipping in through the boys' window, she wondered if Earthsiders missed the games of the gods. Laurel had been shielded for a year and now she was thrust into the midst of an epic war between the brother-gods and the Fates. She hoped the girl had the mettle to persevere. She wished she could have told the Earthsider to believe. *Just believe*.... Because that's what it's going to take.

Belief.

Do I? she mused. *Do I believe enough to abandon this island for the Underworld if it comes to that?*

Time and distance, she reminded herself. Right now she had little left of both. She set aside her thoughts and focused on what was next: Returning Lord Poseidon's island to some semblance of order before she herself set off on an adventure of her master's making.

EIGHTEEN

Laurel awoke to the gentle rocking of *The Balance*.

"Paul." She said his name out loud. It felt at home, warm. It reminded her of lessons in Greek, dancing and eating couscous, lazy night's together, moonlit walks along the beach.

It all seemed normal...natural.

"Poseidon." She said his other name out loud and it conjured up tragic voyages provoked by the god of the seas, wanton lust for sea nymphs, some fragmented memories of a rivalry with Athena—all stories and myths none of which sounded even remotely normal.

Poseidon was a name synonymous with the ocean—her father had paid homage to the god more than once. The name brought images of a white haired merman wielding a trident, commanding the sea. And a singing crab named Sebastian.

She laughed a little at that.

Laurel sat up and slowly peeled herself out of the uncomfortable cot. She was accustomed to a down pillow and a mattress that felt as though she slept on air. Knowing what she knew now that probably wasn't too far from the truth. *What can he do? What are his powers?* Oh for goodness sake he's not superhero. He's a man. He is Paul *and* Poseidon—being a god may be no different than being left-handed—so what's the difference?

But there was a difference. And she wasn't quite sure that she'd made up her mind yet which one she wanted or for that matter, with whom she'd fallen in love. She found her discarded clothing from last night had been replaced with a fresh set. She raised the folded material to let it fall, revealing an elegant floral *peplos.* Paul would have adored her in this. She pulled the garment down over her head. She made the adjustments Paul had spent an afternoon (so long ago) teaching her: turning and pulling in the waist, crossing a quarter tuck—all that she lacked were fasteners for the shoulders. A quick search and she found a pair of brass fasteners as well as beige girdle she used to tie the peplos at her waist. She looked in the mirror and frowned. Not because her black curls lacked their usual bounce or her face strongly suggested she'd been mugged—but because she'd done everything right.

You'll get it, Laurie—it takes time. You're accustomed to val-crow...sygnómi, sorry—Velcro. You see, we are teaching each other...come here, let me show you how easily the pelpos comes off....

She left the cabin quickly and returned topside to a brilliant cobalt sky bereft of clouds. A glove of ocean air embraced her and brought her all the way back to being a five year old girl stepping aboard Dad's ship the first time. His coarse hands hoisting her up above the railing of the Coast Guard cutter where Dad introduced her to the Atlantic Ocean. Looking out now, surrounded by these unfamiliar waters, the feeling of anticipation was the same. *When do I get to go out there, daddy?* That had been her first question that day.

Now, almost thirty-five years later her first question was: When am I going home? And she also wondered, why hadn't Paul just told her the truth? This is *Olympos* after all...*the* Olympos.

She breathed in the Olympian ocean air just the same, the folds of the pelpos ruffling in a passing breeze. *I could use you here, Dad.* She cast out the thought as a net but was sure it would catch nothing. Crossing the freshly scrubbed deck, she looked about for Trutina. She needed him to distract her thoughts, even if only with his three word sentences. She found him whittling away at a gnarled piece of orange wood, a handful of petals of the curious bark lay at his feet. He hummed a new tune, playful and peppy keeping rhythm with each slice of his blade.

"*Kalimera*, Laurel. Did you sleep well?"

"Good morning to you too, Trutina. I don't know. I can't remember sleeping. Maybe it's the first real sleep I've had since Paul died."

"Perhaps." He whistled and whittled.

"Thank you for this," she patted the pelpos and watched his deft hands working a short curved knife over the wood. Though he did not appear to look at his hands, the rhythmic movements reminded her of a potter working clay. There was no distinct shape to the piece of wood yet. The color intrigued her the most, though: a vibrant orange, like an exceptionally bright pumpkin. "What sort of wood is that you're carving?" She took a seat beside him on a squat stool.

"*Ochray*...sunwood. The color is so because Phoebus descends to grace a copse of trees at dusk with a kiss. It grows only on the western shore of..." his pause caught her off guard, though not because he stopped speaking, rather, because she thought he started to smile.

"Please, don't feel that you have to coddle me. I will learn the rules of this place sooner or later." She patted his arm and he jerked back from her; something about the wood had to do with Isa?

"No. It is of no matter." He paused, and subdued his smile; his expression caught between something what looked like regret and...joy?

Laurel decided not to press him. He seemed in an especially pleasant mood, albeit no less peculiar in his mannerisms. Still, he was not the somber and focused man from last night. She moved on, "I am glad you chose this pelpos—the pants and shirt felt...out of place."

Trutina said nothing; his hands had ceased their waltz.

Laurel tried another subject. "Are we close to the second lighthouse? To Athena?" She wanted to work toward the reason she'd even sought him in the first place. But she was reluctant now to bring up Paul's death or his life, if it might amplify Trutina's strangeness.

Trutina spun the wood in the palm of his hand abruptly and began whittling a new section. "Ay-yuh. By tomorrow's dawn we shall reach her shores."

She could not be sure, understandably she had no instruments of measure, no chart by which to gauge her guesses but she felt it in her bones just the same: They'd covered over a thousand miles while she slept. Impossible Earthside, and somehow plausible for her now. Laurel said nothing about it, fearful that to question this man about such things would be an insult. She let him whittle in silence, trying to formulate her questions about Poseidon, the state of current events in Olympos, and about him. "Trutina, I need to know...a few things." There wasn't a delicate way to bring up something like this. No amount of social etiquette training can prepare anyone for how you coerce information about a god from... well, from Trutina.

The Angler did not look up, though his humming had diminished to a murmur. Orange petals of wood curled and dropped to the deck. Last night, his brevity seemed consistent with his curmudgeon exterior. Even in the morning light, surrounded by a magnificent patch of ocean, the man still exuded an air of crankiness. There was something else there, though, that pause and his poorly hidden warm smile all seemed clever evasions of the truth.

"I want to know about Paul...I mean...about Poseidon." She opened her mouth to add a question about him, about Isa.

But a screech from above broke her thoughts. The alert gave her enough time to scramble up and away as a jagged shadow fell across them. Laurel looked up just in time to see a man falling toward them!

She moved, but not quickly enough; the man's body rolled across her and then she was pummeled by his wings. She heard Trutina shouting Grecian curses, while she managed to extract herself out from under the man and his *wings*? Yes! Wings!

"A thousand pardons, Angler; the ship moves more swiftly this close than from up there and the winds—that is the trumpery, tragedy? The trajectory—changed unexpectedly and—oh. Oh foulness, I've bent them again, Da is going to be irate." He pulled and twisted a few of the feathers.

Laurel stared at the handsome boy—not a man. He bore a mop of kinky brown-blond hair splayed out all over his head shadowing murky-brown eyes and an angular nose. He smiled at her and bowed.

"M'lady. I apologize for my cantankerous...oh...scratch

that...no, that's not the word—my audacious entrance. Audacious. Can...cantankerous. Bit of a different there, a bit."

He spoke with a vigorous British accent, his thin lips savoring every word he spoke. He wore an array of colorful clothing from his argyle socks to beige knickers and a bright blue tunic belted by a gold rope all topped by a cherry-red vest riddled with pockets out of which poked all manner of curious objects: eye-bolts, pencils, a pocket watch, zip ties, a pair of glasses and what may well have been a muddied and broken i-Pod.

Trutina collected himself, sliding the knife and wood into a back pocket. "Ay-yuh. You are late, as well." It was not an accusation from the Angler, merely an observation.

"I know, I know—there's a Hades of a storm brewing near Posi's Isle. Can't catch a headwind for a coin or a kiss. Oh. M'lady, my most humblest apologies for your loss, I did not mean the disregard—disrepect?—disregard?—for your feelings. Do you have any food, Trutina?" The boy clapped his hands together and the wings sprouting out of his back withdrew themselves like automatic awnings moving down and in until they appeared like nothing more than a gray and weathered, rough-looking backpack.

"You're Icarus, aren't you?" she blurted out.

His face brightened considerably. "At your service," he flourished a bow, his accent thickening briefly. He met her eyes levelly and said, "and you are she—the capturer of a god's heart. But Posi was wrong—you shine brighter than moonlight upon the ocean."

Laurel blushed now and looked to Trutina who had moved on to the pilothouse. "Be about it," the Angler called down to them. "Our path will find Aeolus' breath soon; Your hands and backbones will be needed."

"He's grumpy...I think." Laurel muttered.

"It seems such. But truth be told I'd wager my wings you remind him of someone." Icarus fiddled through his vest-of-many-pockets.

"Isa..." she whispered. And then more conspiratorially: "His daughter...or wife?"

"Mmm...not in those terms; more like his better half. Have you broken fast?" Icarus scanned the deck and frowned. "Seems not; he doesn't make a good host of late."

"Wait, what do you mean better half?" Laurel watched the Angler's back, more curious than ever about her chauffer.

"Indeed. Trutina! We're going below decks to raid your galley. Would you like a morsel or two?"

"Hunh. I and you have little time for—"

"Right. Got it. Da said Aeolus is restless so your winds may be detained...delayed...delayed? Worry not, Angler. We'll not be long." Icarus took Laurel's hand and guided her below decks. He moved swiftly, nearly skipping through the narrow hallways. He took her past the room she'd slept in, down a half-flight of steps and into a sizeable galley.

NINETEEN

Twin metal tables occupied the center of the room over which hung all manner of pots, pans, and utensils. The walls of the galley were cupboards all around save for an enormous cooler. Icarus did not hesitate in his preparations. "So, you can eat fruit yes?"

Laurel chuckled, "Yes, I can eat fruit, what a strange question."

"Not if you've never met a...you...I mean an Earthsider before." The winged boy rummaged for food.

"Understood. Are there any bananas? Or, ooh, how about oranges?"

Icarus stuffed a strawberry in his mouth and replied, "Of courf Da would want to meet you sooner."

Laurel watched Icarus gathering bowls and fruit, a few pastries, napkins, and two glasses of an opaque vaguely red-orange juice. He spread all of it out across one of the metal tables and motioned for her to join him. "Thank you, Icarus." She smiled around his name.

"What?"

"It's just that you look nothing like I imagined." She gathered up her pelpos and seated herself on a stool across from him.

"Really? Posi talked about me?" he downed a handful of grapes.

"No. In fact I didn't know Paul was Posi...Poseidon until after he died."

Icarus' face darkened. "I'm sorry. I shouldn't keep talking about him; Da tells me all the time he'd like to clockwork my brain so he could readjust the tick-tock of it."

Laurel took his hand and squeezed. "It's okay. I'm not myself either. All of this is quite overwhelming. You, for example—you're...you're *Icarus*."

"Aye. But I'm just the son of Daedulus."

"No, no. You're more than that—you're a legend in my world."

Icarus suddenly looked frightened.

"You flew to the sun and—"

"Stop. Please, I don't fancy that story." The boy buried his face in his glass, downing the entire contents.

"I didn't...I'm sorry. For me, it's a piece of Earthsider mythology. It still sounds weird when I say it." Laurel took his hand again. Icarus stiffened but did not pull away.

"Posi didn't explain any of it, this, *Olympos* did he?"

"I.... No. No, I guess he's hoping I'll fill in the gaps myself. But my mythology and your reality haven't meshed very well. I'm just glad to be going somewhere; maybe I can figure out more of it by the time we get to Athena's island."

"If you promise not to talk about *that myth*, I'll fill you in on what I can."

Laurel studied Icarus closely. His olive-toned skin radiated youthful vigor. He could have been from California or Tennessee but he would definitely be the center of attention, Earthside. He couldn't be older than nineteen, though she suspected he was closer to sixteen. His attire notwithstanding, Icarus did not resonate strangeness like Trutina did. His golden brown eyes glittered and in a few years, he'd be irresistible.

"I'll never speak of it again, Icarus. And yes, I do need your help. I'm lost. Trutina's been polite but nothing more. I know we're headed to Athena's island, strange as that is for me, but I don't know if Paul is alive or dead...and then the Fates and their whole we hate Laurel business...and really I'd like to know this thing from stem to stern and I'm afraid that I'll never manage to find some way home." Laurel hadn't meant to break down but the tears came quietly anyway.

Icarus watched her and said nothing until she'd collected herself. "My Da said you'd be...balderdash, what word did he use? Baffled, buttered...*Bedazzled*! Yes, that's what he said. Da explained that, until you found the second lighthouse, you'd stay bedazzled by the Fates—maybe even longer." Icarus smiled broadly and then inhaled a peach in just a few bites.

"The Fates. I hate them. Especially Mathropos."

"Ah! You and I shall be such good friends. I concur, those witches with switches...no...scissors...switches sounds better—curse the diction—they seek only the betterment of themselves through the destruction of others."

"Mathropos has something more than a switch, I think." She bit off several chunks of banana, suddenly hungry.

"Da would slap me blind for saying this but I imagine Makaisi skinned alive at least once a new moon." He peeled the skin off a grape to demonstrate.

"I don't care for her either. Mira, I'm not so sure about. She seemed, I don't know, forced into all of it. But I'll be glad if I never see any of them again."

Icarus whistled high and long. "So, you've tangled with the Keeper of the Thread?"

Laurel shook her head slowly, "I don't know if tangled quite captures what she did to me. But yes, I know Mathropos all too well." Laurel, finished the banana and devoured several grapes. "I keep trying to make everything that's happened so far fit my reality. It works out alright until I think I feel the sisters touching my Threads, or I picture Paul as Poseidon."

"I'm sorry, m'lady. I'm not very good at explaining things —Da is a master at it. And you're the first Earthsider I've ever met so I'm not entirely sure how to handle you either." He batted a strawberry back and forth between his hands.

"Earthsider. You see what I mean? This is the kind of weird stuff that happens to bad actors on SciFi or to lonely farmer's wives on some Discovery Channel documentary about alien abductions. I'm sitting in the galley of a ship named *The Balance* captain'd by a blind man—don't think I missed that bit of irony, by the way—on an ocean that shouldn't exist talking to a character I studied in a graduate course on World Mythology all the while running away from the Fates because I fell in love with Poseidon."

"When you phrase it that way it certainly sounds like a bard's tale, which I'm partial to. Not Homer though, he found flatulence amusing. Ok, Earthsider...that I can explain. Hand me those bananas and grapefruit please. Laurel scooped up the requested fruit and handed each to Icarus.

"Thank you. Now for my first trick...." Icarus manipulated the fruit as he talked. "This grapefruit is Earth. Mind you, this is not to scale. A lovely globe dangling harmlessly in space chock full of Earthsiders like yourself." He set the grapefruit in the middle of the table. "Now, then, here's the wonky part: Earth is the center...of everything. Got that?"

"You mean the center of the galaxy; the Milky Way?"

"No. Well, yes, that is true—but by no, I mean that's not what I mean. That is I'm not talking about *just* your galaxy. I mean that Earth is the center of *all* of it.

"Da and Posi made this map by which this fruit just doesn't do justice, but they made a map that shows how everything's tied back to Earth. Here, it's something like this." He took eight bananas and laid them around the grape-fruit; their points equidistance around the circumference. "Think of these bananas as lines to other places—not planets, not dimensions, not rips in the space-time continuum. Just other places. And these here, these tips, touch Earth all over."

Laurel stared at what very much resembled a flower which Icarus had formed with the fruit. "The Reef." She said at last.

"Right! The Reef, that's a touch-point. A conclave... convection...Connection. The Reef is a connection to some-place Earthside." He took a banana, peeled it and ate it in a few bites. "Simple, right?"

Laurel traced the arch of a banana. "The Oracle at Delphi?"

"You catch on quick for an Earthsider." He scooped up another banana and consumed it.

"But, center of everything, what else is there?"

"You need to see Da's map, really." He lowered his voice, "I'm not supposed to be sharing too much about it with you."

"Why not? Because I'm an Earthsider?"

"Ehh...sorta...and, Da says it will freak you out."

Laurel sighed. "Well, he's probably right. But...if we're in Olympos now why aren't there centaurs, and chimera, and

Cerberus playing catch with Charon or Zeus himself hurling lightning bolts? How did Poseidon keep all of Olympos quiet for the entire year I lived with him?"

"Has it really been that long? A wonder, that bit of truth. I'd have wagered my wings it was much shorter." He hopped off the stool and paced around the table. "You've never been away from Posi or his island, have you?" His voice sharpened, pushing his tone to almost a falsetto.

"There was no reason to go anywhere; not that I knew there was an anywhere else to go. I was sailing the Mediterranean when I lost my father's ship. Trutina found me and brought me to Paul's island. I just assumed I was somewhere off the western coast of Greece, near Nafsika or Arkudi island. For all I knew Paul Okeanos was best friends with Ari Onassis Scorpios."

"I don't believe Scorpios attends the monthly Olympian meetings."

"I fell in love with Paul, not Poseidon. Now, I don't know anything. I'm talking to Icarus. And not a single moment since Paul's death has made any sense."

Icarus said nothing. He smiled awkwardly, and waited silently.

Laurel wanted to talk. Icarus had uncorked her need to just talk. "Before I left for Greece I was a teacher at Cape Fear Community College and an occasional columnist for the Hatteras Herald. Greek mythology intrigued me, but only because they were *stories*. I probably studied them a little more than most Earthsiders but that still doesn't make up for all of this. Why didn't I know? If it's because Paul tricked me somehow well...I'm not sure I can bear that on top of everything else, Icarus." She blurted out a laugh just saying his name because it wasn't possible, it wasn't real.

"I didn't come here to fall in love with the god of the

oceans. Let alone have an intimate conversation about any of it with you, *Icarus*. But at the same time, I can't help but be awed and amazed—I want to take it all in and make it more real. Except I know that's never going to happen without Paul. So in the end, I don't care about any of this. I'm fighting the urge to quit. To just want to be home so badly I can wish it true." Finally, she'd said aloud what had been skittering around the back of her brain. The same thoughts that had kept her from being involved with her father. The dark thing living in her brain that made sure she wasn't there the day her father died alone. *Quit*, it whispered, *quit this whole business and you can be on your way.*

"I do not have the answers you seek. Posi and Da do not allow me into their private meetings but you'd be surprised how long I can hover over a skylight. Still, what little I do know isn't really going to help you much. I have to say you're doing remarkably well for your first time here—it's a wonder you've kept it together this long! Truth be told, you need to meet my Da. He can explain so much more, show you more. But I'm not supposed to bring you until after...." His voice trailed off.

"After what? After the Fates decide to unravel my Threads fifty-six more times? Or after I've seen Paul's body and said my last goodbye?" She felt like crying but didn't. Instead, she stood up and started pacing.. She watched Icarus as she did. "Does it get easier?" she wondered aloud.

"If you are asking me will things change, all I can say is that they already are. You will feel it soon I suspect. I can see why he is short with you though."

"Who? Paul? He—"

"No. Trutina. You favor her."

"His wife or what did you call her, his better half? I just *lovvvve* unexplained mysteries, may I have another? I tell you what. Why don't we just jump on over to Demeter's pad and discuss an extension on spring and summer?"

Icarus laughed, and patted the seat beside him. "Posi said you were funny. It's what he needed." He drifted off a moment. Then, abruptly, the boy stood and took Laurel by the wrist pulling her to the stairs.

"What do you mean? Hey, slow down—what do you mean it's what Paul needed?"

"Come on. You need a holiday...a vacation...oh which is it? Neither? You need a bird's eye view of this, that's what I think." He ushered her back to the upper deck and directly to the center of the faded mural. "Or, more accurately... appropriately...*interestingly* an Icarus' eye view."

"Icarus, where are we going?" Laurel released the handful of pelpos she'd gathered to keep up with him.

"First, let's do away with the formality...formula? Hmm, peculiar connection there...anyway, my Da's the only one who calls me Icarus. Well, him, Posi, and Trutina—but my friends call my s. Truly, it's far easier and faster to say."

Laurel grinned at the boy. "I don't know if I can do that—"

He frowned at that and she quickly corrected.

"It's not because we won't be friends, Icarus...Icky. It's just that, where I'm from I've only ever known you as Icarus. It'll take some time, okay?"

He brightened up immediately. "Fair enough. Now you're sure you've been here a year? And neither Da nor Posi explained *any* of how all this works?"

"Icarus—eh, Icky, I already told you. I only knew 'Posi' as Paul Okeanos. To me, he was a wealthy Greek with his own island and plenty of time for me. And I can honestly say I've never met your Da."

"Oh you'd remember that if you had." He glanced

around her, behind himself, and up in to the riggings overhead. He shifted her to the right by three steps. "Better."

"Icarus. Stop. Tell me what you meant by Paul needed it. How do 'I favor *her*'. I can't keep up with you if you won't fill me in on the details. Did the Fates do something to my thoughts? Did Paul?" She felt a tremble of fear pass through her bones.

"Let's just let go of all that jumbo-mumbo...mumbo jumbo...ma-ma...mumbo...weird. We'll leave all this—a year, the Reef, not sure the pelpos is the best attire—" he rifled through his vest producing several black bands and in a whirl of cloth and color reduced the elegant flow of her gown to a stylish (if not awkward) pair of leggings and billowy blouse.

"I'm impressed, Icky. What can you do with hair? Never mind—put those away."

"We're set then. We're not going to talk about Posi or Trutina's wife—by the way your hair is raven black and curly, hers was a sort of a wavy midnight—no more, no more, we've got to get on with the good stuff."

Trutina appeared then, regarding them with salty indifference, as he made his way to the pilothouse. Laurel briefly considered calling out to him for help.

"Aeolus hasn't seen fit to blow this way yet so we've the time to indulge in a little sea sighting—mark that, insert homonym...site seeing, right old Angler?"

Trutina said nothing.

Icarus waved at him and chortled lightly. "He's fun isn't he?" The boy repositioned her to face away from the center mast, moving behind her swiftly leaving little time for her to process any of it.

"A few basics rules: do not scream because it is a bit of a shock at first. Two, if you let go you will fall and while, at the risk of sounding a braggart, I am quite fast—I will not be fast enough to catch you before you...which means you could land in the ocean—not sure that's a positive—or you could land on land (land on land? Land...landon? Never mind.) Three, forget everything you're troubled with just for a while, okay? I'm going to help you the best way I know how. By showing you."

"Icarus, I don't follow you. What are you—*oh my God don't you...Noooo!*"

Icarus wrapped his arms up under her armpits and they lifted off the deck. Laurel cut off her scream and slapped her hands to his elbows. The rhythmic *vrriff, vrriff* of Icarus' wings filled the air around them. Her pelpos-now-pantsuit fluttered around her but the boy's bands and tucks held.

"You can open your eyes, Laurel—it's quite beautiful up here." The boy's voice was nearly giddy.

Laurel opened her eyes and looked down.

"Oh Paul...why didn't you just *show* me?"

TWENTY

Icarus hovered a few hundred feet over Trutina's ship, long
enough for Laurel to decide this world held as much beauty
as her own. Nothing obstructed her view of The Reef,
stretching beyond site in either direction like an oceanic
Great Wall of China. Her eyes followed the barrier back
toward Paul's island where she saw a storm brewing there.
She thought of the dilapidated mural on Trutina's ship,
which reminded her of Paul in the silvery light of the moon.
Other memories pinged along this line of thinking but she
could not gather them. Had Paul been trying to tell her about
this all along?

To the north, the direction in which Trutina was presently headed, thick knots and whorls of the blue-gray storm
clouds churned in the sky, preventing her from seeing any
more than endless ocean. But the sky east and west seemed
as blue and infinite as a dream.

"Icarus, this is breathtaking."

He descended, grunting as he spoke. "I'm glad you
appreciate the view. I don't have occasion to bring many
people up here—and Da only allows me to fly this far for

special events because of...that...well...the incident you mentioned earlier." He grunted again, dropping ten feet.

"Icarus, are you ok? If I'm too heavy we can—"

"No! Burden me, no, you're not too heavy. It's just too soon after flying all the way here, which is why I had to eat but it's ok, really. I just want you to have some...space... peace? Yes, peace." His words came through the vice of his lips with considerable effort. "Over there of course you see The Reef...and...to the north, beyond that rather nefarious looking storm...*urrgh*, which I'm certain the Fates installed... out...of...spite...that is where we trek at the moment... Athena's Island."

They dropped abruptly and Laurel caught a scream in her throat. "Let's head back, Icarus—I don't think this is the best idea." She tried not to kick her legs, fearful she'd drop them both into the ocean.

Indeed, the world below them was all ocean: green and blue, dark and choppy—in some spots she could make out beige amoebic shapes she decided were sandbars. In other areas she saw swift moving dark auras to which she pointed and Icarus replied: "Nymphs most likely, but they could be schools of kelpi. We're too far out for them to be sirens and the mermaids are extinct."

"Mermaids?"

She felt him laughing and slapped his arms.

"I'm sorry, I couldn't resist. There are no mermaids here in Olympos; but there are many wonders here I hope to show you, if there be time. If Trutina allows that is...we are still at least a day from Athena's island and there is so much... so...much."

"I only want to know about Paul, Icarus. But let's not discuss that up here—I don't want to crash down into some...*kelpi*? Is that what you called them?"

"Hedge room."

"What? Where?"

He laughed heartily. "No, no...heh—where...that's a good one. We are currently functioning within Hedge Room at the moment."

"I don't follow you, Icar...Icky."

He fluttered, dipped, but managed to move them along, following the wake of *The Balance*, now less than half a league ahead of them.

"How many girls do you fly around in hopes of stealing a kiss?"

"You are the first. That is...I mean I don't want to steal anything from you..."

"Icky one, Laurel one." She laughed easily and it surprised her.

"Ah, the game is afoot...on...afoot? Alright, touché I believe your speakers of French say. Da doesn't appreciate hedge room—so flying around with anything but my satchel is forbidden."

"Hedge room. You mean, you push the limits?"

"Well you have to believe that there are limits to push them I suppose. And I don't, so I can't. But there is *always* hedge room."

Laurel wanted to turn and give him a look she'd received from her father on numerous occasions when she questioned his authority on boats, or knots, or the seven seas.

"I know, I know—I don't need to see you to get it but it really makes exquisite sense...exciting...exact? Hmm..." he trailed off in a mumbling dialogue with himself.

Laurel felt herself embracing his energy; a big sister reunited with her little brother after summer camp. Icarus had the right combination of idiosyncrasies and sincerity making him that much more adorable. "I cannot believe we're discussing this up here."

"It's majestic isn't it? It's one of my eleven favorite places to be."

"Eleven? You're a mess Icky, a mess."

"Oh, well, everyone I know seems to have this penchant for units of five or ten—Da, Posi even. So I don't like to live in other people's boxes—which brings us back again to hedge room."

Laurel felt her smile reach her eyes.

"Everything Da invents has his perceived limitations to it. That's his box and he's happy in that. He has his own degree of error—those are his words. I add my hedge room to those limitations and I know how far I can go before I've broken, burned, shattered, shredded, or killed myself."

"So, right now for example—your wings. Your Da tells you that they'll not allow any more than a certain amount of weight. Your hedge room buffers that to compensate for me?"

"Yes, marvelous!" He swooped low and spiraled counter-clockwise eliciting a sharp shrill of surprise from her.

"Ok, let's not do that again. I don't think Trutina would appreciate a rain of vomit."

Icarus evened out their flight path and brought them to within fifty feet above *The Balance*.

She could have hovered above the ocean for the rest of the day and not cared. She tilted enough to catch a glimpse of the storm brewing over the island she'd called home for a year. It didn't seem as fierce as Icarus' tale suggested. Looking ahead of *The Balance*, however, their course would lead them close enough to the ugly storm for them to feel it in the currents. But for now, things seemed okay. In fact, being up here away from the water ironically made her feel closer to Paul. *When you awaken, this body you know will be dead and I will be again in the diamesos traveling to Anaktoro where the Allagi will occur.* He'd said that last night? No, two nights ago, right? Yes, she had been on the beach the morning of his funeral and then awakened here a morning later. *Find me, Laurie,* he'd whispered. And then he died. But then how did Trutina know...?

"Damn you Paul...Bring us down. Icky! Bring us down *now!*"

"Aye, but are you alright?" He descended quickly and with considerable grunting, swaying, and dipping.

She couldn't speak, not yet. She was forming the connections as they drew closer which seemed to take an hour. Icky tried his best to prevent them from dropping unceremoniously but he could not maneuver easily and ended up dropping her five feet above the main deck. She compensated readily enough, rolled out of the fall and nearly landed in the middle of the mural. The boy fluttered up over the pilot house, waved at Trutina and landed on the bow railing, perching like a partially feathered bird.

"Trutina." Laurel called to him, breathlessly.

He did not turn from his post.

"When did Paul send you to 'rescue' me?" She doubted the blind Angler would see her air quotes but she knew he heard them. She felt a thrum in her bones, every fiber of her body urged her to run up beside him and shake the blindness from his eyes.

The Angler did not turn as he spoke, "The answer will not be what you wish it to be. Nor will knowing aide you in your journey."

"Damn it old man, can't you just give me a straight answer? This isn't already the freakiest thing that's ever happened to me without your stupid cryptic responses."

If he watched her she could not tell, though she was sure he was listening. She felt something fragmenting inside, felt a jolt of fear at the sensation but she welcomed it just the same.

What are you doing? She scolded herself. She didn't know. Didn't care.

Trutina's expression did not change. Laurel wielded her rising ire like a morning star.

"I'm *not...from...**here!*** I didn't get a rule book that explains how things are supposed to work! I didn't ask to be brought to Paul's island—YOU TOOK ME THERE, DAMNIT! So I think you can try answering my questions. Directly, this time—and I think you can stop this ship until we have things straightened out."

Are you listening to yourself? She was but couldn't stop it.

Silence from the Angler, although she thought she saw his face tighten. The owl's head pendant slapped against her chest as she ratcheted up, but she wasn't about to seek solace from the man-god who'd tricked her.

Icarus mouthed something to her, his face ruddy and pinched with the effort, but she ignored him too.

"Are you going to answer me? Are you going to do more than stand there?" Laurel felt hot and senseless—or maybe just *all senses* at once.

"Your words bring—"

She cut him off, "Stop before you get started with more of your verbal analgesic. I don't need placating or coddling. I'm not your wife who's probably more than capable of deciphering your cryptic grunts and gestures. But, honestly, I'm not surprised *Isa* left you if all she ever got for attention were blank stares and crazy-stupid riddles!"

Trutina slapped her sharply, the sting dissipating through

her face; the ire of her words resonating in her head though she didn't recall speaking them.

"Ouch...I kinda figured that was gonna happen." Icarus tight-rope-walked along the railing past the pilot house to the rear of the ship.

Laurel's eyes blurred with tears of pain and for a long moment she could not speak.

"I am neither your slave nor your seer, *Earthsider*. I am not here to entertain you or provide you with the secrets of this world. I owed Poseidon a debt and that debt *alone* shall be paid. But if you ever mention Isoropia again, I will tether you to anchor of *The Balance* and drag you the remaining distance to Athena's isle!"

His jaw crushed the final words to silence.

Laurel could only muster a meager and raspy, "I'm sorry". She turned and wanted to rush off in shame. Instead, she made herself leave a gracefully as she could muster.

Whywhywhywhy rattled in her brain like a loose nut on a rusty fan.

Just keep moving, she admonished herself.

Got yourself a dervish, lil'fin. Her father trying to explain a mood she'd been in when she was nine or fifteen or twenty-six.

Yeah, that's what it was. A dervish.

She kept moving, feeling their eyes on her back but certain that if she turned, neither of them would be looking.

TWENTY-ONE

Mathropos paced.

Makaisi and Mira had finally been dispatched to deal with the Earthsider but their absence had done nothing to diminish her pacing.

Or her fear.

"Bah!" she hated the sound of her voice bouncing off the deteriorating marble walls. She stopped her pacing, her knees continued shaking.

She knew she would soon have to go back to finish her talk with the ocean-god but doing so now would only reveal to him the affect he'd had on her composure. "Pathetic creature," she muttered. She resumed her pacing to still her obstinant knees. The time would come when others would shake in her presence; when *all* of Olympos would tremble at the mere mention of her name.

"As it had once been," her voice came back to her again. She didn't realize she'd even spoken aloud.

She blamed the brother-gods. Their meddling had caused this. Their inability to see that the war had been lost to them decades ago only exasperated the situation...

provoked the necessity of consuming more threads than she'd ever held!

She would endure, she knew. "I am the Keeper." Again she spoke out loud without meaning to but this time the words did not come back to her.

Mathropos looked at her surroundings and realized she had left the marble hall and entered some dark alcove. But there were no alcoves such as this in the House of Zeus, none that she knew of and she had become intimately familiar with Anaktoro. "If this is some of your trickery again Poseidon I shall bring your suffering to a level heretofore never experienced by a god!"

There was no answer.

There was nothing. Just blackness around her.

Cautiously, she reached out to feel the darkness and her hands immediately touched rough thatching. Swiftly, Mathropos moved along the wall to what she hoped would not be—

But the sconce was there, beside the table which held her small collection of trinkets, books, and baubles. Her hands trailed over the items. She resisted the urge to clutch the last one: an amber scarab. Plain in its design, the details of its body worn away over time, she had not held it since her days as a girl, playing in the shadows of the Theosophane....

You've done it again, foolish old woman.

She swept her hand over the table scattering the treasures around the darkness of the room. With a thought, she stepped out of the room of her childhood and back into the marble hall within the House of Zeus.

She did not waste a moment, striding into the chamber where the ocean-god hung suspended from the ceiling over the only thing that could revitalize him. The only thing in all of Olympos capable of saving his life. She climbed up onto his back using his own Threads to do so and jerked them out of his being with such force it would have killed a normal man, mayhap crippled a demi-god.

His screams reverberating off the walls even managed to stir the waters below them.

"Good. You know now that I mean to end this." She could almost taste his Threads, their majestic flavor would do more than satisfy her. A single fiber would—

"Sister?" Mira watched her from below, her fat form repulsive and deceptive.

Mathropos released Poseidon and dropped to stand beside the woman. "What now, *sister*. Can you not see that I am busy?"

"Indeed. It seems you were about to take matters into your own hands. A decision such as that warrants a conference with Makaisi and I, wouldn't you agree?"

She detested Mira's voice. So coddling as to be syrup. "Do not lecture me, Mira. I am the Keeper."

"Are you?" Mira strolled away, glancing up at the unconscious god of oceans as she went.

Mathropos settled herself before following. "I will not play your asinine game, Mira. What is it you want? Why did you interrupt me?"

Mira did not answer immediately. She continued to walk around the immense pool of sea water, appearing to admire the details in the tile or the artwork lining the walls. "I thought perhaps you might be interested in knowing your machinations have begun to pay off. The change has begun. The *Meliai* have returned."

Mathropos' grin cut the brittle flesh of her face like a gash. "And you doubted me. Bah! I will see to our young charge then. You remain here. Mira, I am speaking to you! You will remain here and await Poseidon's return to consciousness." She moved swiftly toward Mira, closing the distance before the woman even knew she'd moved at all. "You will do *nothing*. Do you hear me? Do not speak to him. Do not look at him. I swear upon the Weave if you so much as cough in his direction I will unravel you."

That threat stung her, Mathropos could see it in her sister's cherubic face. The normally mellow glow flared a deep crimson and fires sparkled in her eyes a moment. "I see that you recall the last time I reminded you of who I am. Good. Do not cross me, sister. I shall return before nightfall."

Mathropos paused a moment, feeling some slight tension on the Theosophane she'd never felt before. The Threads within her body undulated spastically, almost erupting from between her breasts. *I am the Keeper*, she repeated for the thousandth time, willing the unruly strands to settle. *I must take more to tame them; if only I could pluck a filament from the Earthsider. Oh how succulent the Threads of an Earthsider!* She stopped short of salivating. This would not do. She would need to seize control of herself if she was to seize control of Olympos. Matters would have to be expedited, certain players within this game would need to be...unraveled...but all for the good of Olympos.

She could go to Father, of course. Directly into the Theosophane. *I carry so many Threads now, what would their presence do to the Grand Weave?*

Mira watched her curiously, a smirk playing at the corners of her mouth.

Mathropos moved through the Weave and through Mira. She stopped just behind the fat woman and grabbed deep, holding hair and scalp and whispered: "You may think you have *nothing* left to lose sister but I know your secrets. *All. Your. Secrets.* If need be, I will reveal you to Father and, mark me, his punishment will far overshadow my removal of your daughter."

A whimper blubbered from her thick face.

Mathropos released Mira with a chuckle. Gather more Threads, end the game, reweave the whole of it as she saw fit and then she could rest again. With that thought she left the House of Zeus in search of satisfaction.

TWENTY-TWO

Mira waited for the pain in her scalp to recede before she drifted up beside Poseidon. She stroked his sweat soaked head, humming a lullaby. "I know this does little to ease your pain, but I promise you it will soon be a memory."

The god of oceans did not move.

She did not expect him to. The pain Mathropos had inflicted upon him should have killed him. She had seen it done before, her sister's limitless wrath destroying a life without compassion or thought.

Fortunately, Mira had seen to it that such tragedies could not happen again. There were some small benefits to being The Spinner. Nonetheless, the danger of failure remained too immediate for her to remain here much longer. She had an eternal amount of work to attend to, beginning with the watchdogs upon Poseidon's island. Spinning their threads had been painless, but laying them out for her prey to read or rather misread proved to be a work even Father would have considered doomed.

The god of oceans stirred and Mira soothed him again by stroking her fingers along his naked back. "Not yet," she whispered to him. She caressed the ceiling above him, too, taking care to avoid the threads but coaxing water droplets from the skin of the ceiling just the same.

"It is not much, I know." she whispered.

Nothing perceptible changed in the god, but she knew he had. "Soon."

Mira sighed as she descended to the floor. She adjusted her shawl and robes unnecessarily, stalling she knew. Around her the Weave showed itself as an infinite web of amber strands: Some pulsing brilliantly, others flickering spastically, each one of them born of her womb. She caressed several thousand of them with one pass of her hand, smiling as she did so, infusing them with a sigh. A sigh that would translate into good tidings, simple joys, perhaps even luck.

"Olympos knows we need a good deal more of that, don't we?" she chuckled, her mirth reverberating back to her off the marble walls. Looking up at her sister's artwork she could not help but be impressed. Using the god's own Threads coupled with the Threads of those he'd betrayed, laced with a touch of the few he'd ever loved. Why the tapestry simply glowed with its own majestic, tragic intricacy.

Mira turned away from the hypnotizing pattern, settling herself in for what needed to be done. *Sometimes you must shake the Weave to see if, indeed, the stitches will hold.* She turned, content and focused, and stepped away from the House of Zeus toward Poseidon's Island.

TWENTY-THREE

As a girl, Amynta knew she was destined to become an *oikonomos*. The line of women in her family who served the gods as *oikonomos* stretched back to the beginning of memory. To serve the gods in this manner did not come without blessings or burdens. An *oikonomos* would never go hungry, but could starve for want of release from the pressures and pains of serving. She knew of a few who embraced cowardice rather than face the work; to bring such shame upon the name of one's family? Amynta could not fathom it. Better to do the work and be done with it than condemn your family to ruin and dishonor.

And yet here she was, stalling, finding work to do before doing the work that needed the doing most.

Not stalling, she scolded herself, preparing *to do the work.*

She could hear her mother's voice correcting her: *Amy, you'll not clear the dust by thinking about it. Get about yer work now girl.* Throughout her girlhood, she'd always been a bit of a day dreamer, no harm in that. In fact, her father often encouraged such mental sojourns. But her mother, always the pragmatic one, did not deign herself to such baseless behavior. *Day dreams lead to nightmares*, she was fond of prophesizing.

Amynta never found such to be true, but growing up in her mother's shadow she dared not test her theories. A mother herself now, Amynta had found a meaningful balance between allowing the boys' their flights of fancy while anchoring them in seeing the work be done when it twas to be done.

"Still stalling," she muttered. Not so much stalling now for she'd made her rounds, some twice and all was in order. Winter stocks were sufficient. Diona and Lavail, a pair of girls apprenticed to her, were more than capable of overseeing what duties remained on the island. Though she worried for Lavail, a softheaded girl of thirteen who fancied herself a pretty for Ulgos. Three times this month she'd had to shoo the girl about her business, telling her to save her moon eyes for a boy closer to her age. Diona, on the other hand, that child would be *oikonomos* before her thirtieth birthday, Amynta was certain of it. And what a feat that would be! She herself had been but a day over thirty-three.

She hoped the girl would have the chance.

She hoped for herself she would at the least see another sunrise. If she be lucky, and the gods willing, she would dance with her boys at her fifty-second *haroumena genethlia* or what did the Earthsider call it? Her birthday?

Thoughts of the Earthsider inevitably brought her back to thoughts of her husband.

"Vettias," she whispered his name, fearful that the veil had thinned as of late. Deeply concerned that the meddling of the Fates had somehow weakened Lord Hades grasp on the Underworld. Such was not true, she knew, but none-theless, she dared not raise the ire of her deceased husband's spirit.

Amynta finished folding the linens that did not need folding.

"I am stalling," she admitted.

The early afternoon light crept downward, pulling her shadow along with it as the sun crept toward the horizon. *Be about it then,* her mother's voice intoned. *Take heed, Amyntroula,* Vettias would whisper, *some storms start inland.*

Amyntroula. Little Amynta.

Only Vettias had ever called her that, and today she missed his sweetness more than she had in over five years.

"Get to the work," she scolded herself.

There was nothing left to attend on this island. Diona would take charge, Lavail would follow. Or everything would collapse in her absence and though she'd appease Lord Poseidon's wishes, she'd become a disgrace among her sister *oikonomos.*

She listened for any advice from her mother or her late husband. None came and she knew she could delay her departure no longer.

Poseidon's oikonomos gathered the few items she'd need on her journey, tucking them away in her *sakido platis,* her backpack as Laurel would name it. And she wondered what Vettias would have made of the Earthsider. Would he have kept his distance or shared his awful jokes? Would he have encouraged her to bed Poseidon or condemned her love of a god?

"Stop this drifting girl," she said in her mother's voice.

"Aye," she replied in her own.

Get to the work, see it done.

She laid her hand over her abdomen, checking for the object hidden beneath her *stolla*. Confirming its presence, Amynta stepped away from the huts and faced northwest. She could not see her destination and though she rarely doubted Lord Poseidon on most matters, she wasn't certain she could reach Athena's island ahead of the Earthsider. *You are well-versed in the equestrian arts, yes?* Lord Poseidon had asked her.

Of course. Her father made certain his daughters knew all there was to know about horsemanship from husbandry to hostling.

What of the winged-breed?

Pegasi.

In her lifetime, she'd only ever watched others ride them, never had any care to mount one herself—not for the fear of flying, but of falling to her death because the beast might decide to corkscrew through a cloud, throwing her off at a deadly altitude.

If it be thy wish, I will ride.

It truly would be the only way for her to overtake *The Balance* ahead of the Earthsider.

"And here I am again talking about the work instead of doing it. Be about it, Amynta."

One last bit of work to see to: Bringing Oli and Harlan to the girl Ellera.

Amynta took a deep, slow breath.

She closed her eyes and brought an image of Vettias to mind. His kind infinitely brown eyes, the scars on his left hand from a childhood injury, the way he cupped her face in his hands before kissing her.

"Stop this drifting, girl." She admonished herself. "Be about your business."

It took less time than she thought to say goodbye to the boys. But that was good. Good that they did not know what lay ahead for their mother.

Now, to the Pegasus and then Athena's island.

TWENTY-FOUR

Laurel held the owl's head pendant before her eyes, glaring at it. She lay on the uncomfortable cot, back against the wall, legs propped up, alone in her remorseless room.

A knock on the cabin door.

She didn't answer.

"M'lady, it's me. Icarus?"

"It's fine. Come in." She did not look at him.

Silence took up the remaining space in the cabin.

"She died." Icky offered. He had recessed his wings and removed the coat of many things. He fidgeted with his backpack, settled his hands into a pocket but they took flight up along the door jam.

Laurel's heart had no feeling. *I'd be surprised to feel any beat. Why did I act that way? What did I expect Trutina to say?* Especially when she already knew the answer.

Paul knew all along what was going to happen. He knew because he's not Paul, he's Poseidon. And Poseidon tricked her and put her on this path. Not out of love but out of self-preservation. She dropped her head into her hands, the pendant swung like a noose.

"...isn't exactly accurate." Icarus paced out of the cabin and into the hall.

"I'm sorry, Icky, what? I was only half-listening. I'm chewing on my guilt and confusion, wishing I had my old friend Jack Daniels right here beside me."

"Were you two close?

"What?

"You and your friend Jack Daniels?" he re-entered the cabin and she motioned for him to sit beside her on the bunk.

"Yeah. Too close for too long. What the hell happened to me up there, Icky? God I was a giant bitch to Trutina."

"It's alright, m'lady. As my Da often says if we don't rattle the clockwork now and then how will we ever know and appreciate the sound workmanship? What I was saying is that 'died' is not entirely the best way to describe the fate of Isoropia. She was, mmm rescinded—no, too many syllables; umm remanded...remoooo....Removed! Aye, that's the stretch of it! She was Removed and that's nine times worse than death."

Laurel looked into the boy's alarming golden-brown eyes. "Oh. I didn't...I'm such a terrible person."

"Terribly uninformed perhaps, but you are not terrible inside." He gave her an uneven smile and she could not help but smile back.

"She didn't die then, you said. What is Removed?" but even as she said it she knew it had to do with the Fates.

"I do not understand the process, no one does. But death and Removal send you to two very different places. Death wins you a trip to one of the various planes in the Under-world. Removal sends you to...um...nowhere."

Laurel took a deep breath and tried not to think about her father. Or a Jack and Coke. "So," she let the breath go, "How is it the Fates get to make the rules in Olympos? Don't they answer to the gods? Never mind, stupid question—they're the Fates, right?"

"Every denizen of Olympos lives by rules by which they are bound, that is the way of it. The Fates can do much the gods cannot, true, but they too are bound by rules. Are you hungry?" he abruptly asked.

"No, not reall—" but he was already out and headed to the galley.

He returned a moment later clutching a fistful of fruit. "I wish I had answers for you, m'lady. I am truly sorry for being such an awful tour guide, especially since this is your first time here in Olympos."

"It's not your fault, Icky. I'm the crazy Earthsider who doesn't know shit about Olympos...probably because of the Fates." She mumbled under her breath. "I cannot believe I said all of that to Trutina. I just felt hate, and not necessarily toward him. I've never felt anything like that before." She lied, doubting she'd ever be able to explain to this boy the dark abyss of guilt and regret she carried over her father's death. She changed topics quickly lest she fall back into that abyss again. "Tell me about her, Isoropia." Laurel turned to sit with her legs off the bunk, something fluttered at the back of her mind; a thought like a moth trapped between the window and screen.

Icarus' face darkened, his voice no longer as jubilant, the fruit forgotten. "Mathropos Removed her."

Laurel waited but the fluttering settled. "I don't know if that's what Mathropos was trying to do to me on Paul's beach but it felt like she was between me and my soul."

"Aye, they're quite adept at their thread-work. M'lady, I..." but he stopped.

Laurel looked at the winged-boy. He looked afraid.

The *Balance* rose and fell in a constant, comfortable,

familiar rhythm that made Laurel long to be aboard Dad's ship, *The Ghost*. Aboard her father's ship, she had her home and all the things that had made life bearable after his death. But that wasn't entirely true—it wasn't until almost a year after her father had passed that she'd found the courage to sever ties and make the trip he'd spent over sixty years planning without ever actually sailing. All of those memories and excuses now lay beneath the waters of the Mediterranean Sea; the list of items impossible to replace began rolling through her head, like reels of a slot machine ringing painfully in her head. And then the fluttering thought returned, dashing itself again and again against the screen.

What? She reached out to the thought.

It faltered to a brooding rest in a place she could not quite reach. She knew it was Paul trying to reach her, she felt it in her bones. She took hold of the pendant and the thought fluttered excitedly and then vanished only to be replaced by something else trying to get out. A wave of nausea ushered itself through her abdomen.

"M'lady? Are you getting sea sick?"

"No...it's something else." She squeezed the pendant and waited. The fluttering thought, whatever it was, could not get in until the other thing was gone.

"I shall fetch you some fresh water." He stood to leave.

"No, really. I'm fine...it's a headache, that's all." She caught the boy's brilliant and piercing eyes. "No, that is a lie." She hugged her legs to herself.

Icarus arched an eyebrow and bit into a pear.

"There's something happening in here," she spoke carefully as she tapped her forehead.

Icarus listened.

"I think Mathropos did something to me on the beach in

the shadow of Paul's lighthouse." She felt the other thing quake. "I don't know how to describe it."

Icarus sat beside her. "From the outside, it appears that you are either getting seasick or deathly ill or both."

Laurel closed her eyes and did a little mental poking around. "It feels like she put something at the back of my brain," she described it to the boy.

"Can you flick it away like a bug?"

"I don't think so...I think it's going away on its own the further away we get from Paul's island. And I think once it does, Paul will take its place." She opened her eyes again. "I'm certain of it."

Icarus had finished the pear. "You believe Lord Poseidon to be alive?"

"Yes," she said emphatically. "I think he's hurting, though. I don't know. It's a fuzzy thing that comes and goes but until the other thing is gone...." She trailed off as she felt the other thing quivering, sending another wave of nausea through her gut. "It doesn't want to leave," she said and almost threw up. "Oh—no, no...I can't—I've never been seasick in my life and I've been on rougher seas—" she swallowed down another surge of nausea, barely able to contain the retching. *Go away, go away, go away* she willed it to obey but it remained unchanged.

"Perceived limitations." Icarus declared, casually flexing his wings.

"What are you talking about?" The thing in her brain was opening or melting or blossoming. Yes, it was about to fully bloom and when it did—*The closer you'll be to remembering what you did to him, how you abandoned him*—no!

"M'lady, I'm not an expert on the side effects an Earthsider might experience after an encounter with the Fates, but

I do know that you're suffering from your perceived limitations'."

Laurel steadied her swaying body against the wall. The whispered provocations had abated but she still wanted to scream. The fluttering thought remained at a distance.

"Do you recall our discussion during our aerial jaunt earlier?"

Laurel rubbed her eyes, trying to assuage the rolling waves of nausea. The other thing in her brain had not yet reached its peak. "Yes, hedge room, you called it?"

"Aye. In this moment, you believe you've reached your limitations so why go any further, hm? You're living in your own little box labeled 'Earthsider: Safe Keeping' and you're comfortable with that. All of a sudden, somethin' kicks over that box and all your goodies are scattered across the archipelagos of Olympos. Can't say that wouldn't make me question my own eyes had I never seen such before. But you're ignoring your *own* hedge room, that's the stretch of it. Why poke around and see if there's any other way to go—it all ends the same anyway, right?" The boy's voice had taken on a considerably adult tone, though he could not keep his smile in check for long.

Laurel felt herself wishing she'd met Icarus two years ago. His positive energy was infectious. It held off the old desire to settle all of this with a bottle. A touch from Paul would be better, though. *Are you there?* She pushed the thought out but found no response. "You know," she caught Icarus' warm brown eyes, wide and limitless, his face resonated an eagerness she had once seen in her father's eyes when he talked about sailing *The Ghost,* once and for all, to Greece. "Never mind, you wouldn't understand. Stupid whispers." Laurel caught herself rocking steadily from one foot to the other, her father's voice drifted up from the depths saying *You're doin' that jig again; yer Laurel Waltz ya called it...what's got you* flusterpated, *girl? A boy? School?*

"You are probably correct, m'lady, I wouldn't understand stupid whispers. But does that change how you'd feel if you said it anyway?"

Laurel took the boy's hand in hers. "My dad would have liked you. You don't think like a sheep, he'd say, and that's good for a boy your age." She did her best impression of her father's gravelly baritone voice: "Too many sheep got no problem given up their coat followin' their buddy to slaughter, never asking why." She smiled but it left her face as quickly as it appeared. The other thing, the taint left by Mathropos, continued to bloom, sending dark thoughts along every runnel of her brain. "I miss him, Icky; I miss them both. You are so right. I *do* need to know my hedge room. I need to know this place like I know Earthside. I worry that the shit's gonna hit the fan before that happens though."

Icarus laughed uproariously. "Oh, you and my Da are two cogs in a clock! He is known for saying When the dung heap meets the dirt, you'll be sorry you forgot your boots."

She could not help herself and laughed with him. "Thank you for that. I needed a good chuckle."

"At your service, m'lady", he gave his best regal address, bowed and dropped to one knee.

"It helps me to just stop wishing for things to go back to how they were before Paul died. When he was just Paul. Not Paul *and Poseidon* the ancient Greek god of the oceans. Ok, you can stop kneeling, Icarus." He didn't move. "Sorry, I mean, you may arise good sir knight."

The boy rose as gracefully as the cramped quarters would allow and said, "I can't say I understand everything happening in your noggin, Laurel. As Da explains it, I spend too much of my mind on what's not more than what is. But you have my oath that I shall see this thing through with you to the end, wing to wing."

"I like that: Wing to wing. That's a good catch phrase for you. You make the weirdness of all this bearable, you know that?"

Icarus grinned and blushed.

"I think your Da and my father would had gotten along quite well." She laid her hand on the pendant hoping to feel the fluttering thought. She rolled the silver head of the owl between her thumb and forefinger. Despite the fact that nothing came to her, she found the gesture soothing just the same. "I have to decide to make this important. That's what my Dad would have told me. I can't return to Paul's island and I sure as hell can't go back home—no ship, no job—I don't even have a place to live or money." She laughed.

Icarus tilted his head and furrowed his brow.

She took a deep breath, repeating what her dad often said in times like these: "It is funny, in a way. If you can't laugh it away at least—"

"Laugh for the day," Icarus finished the line.

"What did you just say?" She sat bolt upright.

"It's a common parcel, particle...phrase!" He inched back from the bed toward the doorway.

"No, it's not." She moved toward him. "How did you know?"

Icarus' grin was wide and fake. "I just happen to be a sooth seer and it came to me in my mind."

"Bullshit." Laurel gripped him by the forearms. "How did you know that phrase?"

Icarus' voice stuttered behind his teeth. "I-th-wh"

"There's no way you could have ever heard my father *say* those words. And I know for a fact that there's only one place you could have seen them. So unless you've been to the bottom of the Mediterranean, tell me how the hell did you know those words?"

"Because I read them on the way here." Icarus blurted out.

"Wh-wait. What?" Laurel moved her hands to his shoulders as much to brace herself as to keep him from darting out of the cabin.

"I wasn't supposed to tell you, let alone give it to you until we'd reached Athena's island. But I believe it is time. And, the truth of it is, I like you too much to keep hiding it from you."

Laurel braced herself as Icarus rummaged through his pants pockets. Her left hand made its way absently to the owl's head pendant in preparation.

"It's here, I promise you. Just so many...tiny...unusual... ouch!..that one is sharp. Ah! He asked me to protect you with this...or protect this for you? I can't recall." He produced a battered, caramel brown leather-bound journal that she had expected to never see again. He held it out to her and she wept softly and easily.

"It's Dad's journal...his floatplan. Icarus...Icky.... Wh... wh.." she couldn't form words. She did not want to touch it because it might undo everything. "No." she heard herself saying, doubting the validity of what was right in front of her. "No, I can't. I...there's no way—NO WAY you can have this! It went down with The Ghost. Everything went down with Dad's ship."

Icarus held her father's floatplan out to her atop both palms. "Posi said that you had to have it by the time we reached Athena's island—but not too early. I'd say we're close enough. Here, I've read a few passages; very interesting man your father. He loved you as much as he did the sea."

She reached out hesitantly, certain that upon contact she

would forget everything and wake up face down in the sand dunes which surrounded her father's home in Ocracoke. "Icky, I...I don't know how...what else did he say to you?" Her hands hovered over the book, preparing to receive the last thing she had left of her father.

"Only that it meant a lot to you—certainly more than my life. Storms and wings...strings?...swings?...got to remember that—storms and wings do not mix well. I'm not exactly sure how birds do it, different sort of hedge room I suppose. I wonder, though, if just a bit of tweak to the—"

"Icky. Icarus." Laurel placed both hands on the sides of the boy' face to still the turbulence of his mouth. "May I?" she tabled her hands palms up.

Icarus laid the journal in her hands.

The book touched her skin with a spectral sigh only she could hear and feel. Laurel traced the black brand of the Coast Guard sigil, twin anchors crossed beneath a life ring and shield with *Semper* above and *Paratus* below . "You were always ready, Dad. Always." She held the journal in front of her for a long while.

Icarus said nothing, and if not for the rocking motion of *The Balance*, he would not have moved at all.

Laurel would not let herself cry. Not until this was over. All of it. Getting to Athena's Island, reuniting with Paul.... She forced her thoughts to halt. No more. She clutched the journal against her chest and closed her eyes. "Show me Vegas," she whispered and flipped to a page. She opened her eyes and smiled. "Jackpot," she whispered.

Icarus looked at her curiously.

"It's a game my Dad and I would play when I was young. He'd ask me to plot a course with him to some place exciting, unique, or exotic. I couldn't think of anywhere and

I was only ten—we were living in Florida at the time, Station Miami. So I said, why not Vegas?

"He laughed and told me that was a marvelous idea and proceeded to plot a course—all by water—to Las Vegas. From time to time when I was down or lost he'd hand me a chart book or sometimes even the floatplan and he'd say, *Show me Vegas!* I'd flip open the book—it didn't even really matter where and he'd say, Jackpot, lil'fin. Jackpot."

Laurel closed the journal and laid it on the bed. She circled her arms around Icarus and gave him a long hug to which he relented and returned the embrace. "I still don't know why Paul did this—" she started to say and then stopped, eyes locked on the journal.

"What's wrong?" he stepped back.

"Paul gave this to you? Gave it to you in person?" her voice thinned to breaking.

"Well, not technically *in person*. Posi showed up at Da's but of course Da wasn't there which was alright since it wasn't m'Da he wanted to see."

The wheels in her brain were spinning. She hoped though she dared not ask what she really wanted to know.

"He came upon the subject directly and told me to retrieve the floatplan from a very secret place."

Laurel swallowed back the dryness in her throat. "Icky, did you get this from a ship? From the captain's quarters of a ketch a few feet shorter than Trutina's ship?"

"Well—again—not technically from an actual ship although there was a ship in the painting which hid the area from out of which I retrieved the book. What are you about, here? You're not making much sense and frankly the look on your face suggests you're contemplating a rash course of action."

"The Lighthouse." Laurel shook her head. "I should

have stayed in the lighthouse, I might have...." But then she realized that Paul knew her far too well. He knew she wouldn't stay, knew that she'd end up here—he knew all of this before she knew any of the truth.

"I hope you are not going to ask what you look like you're going to ask. If it's all the same to you, m'lady, I'd much rather not fly back there into the storm. It's a bit brutal on these wings."

"As dry as the day I found it, you know. I'm having a hard time not hating Paul for this, Icky. And yes, if I thought we could, I'd slap a saddle and bridle on you and fly you back to the island myself."

"Oh. That's an unpleasant image; although the idea of a carrier harness of some sort to enable the transport of passengers does sound like a rather interesting idea."

Laurel reached for the floatplan, hugged it—made certain it was truly real, and then laid it back down the bed. She took Icarus in her arms again. "I'm not angry with you. I'm sorry; this is the last thing I expected so when I saw it I thought maybe he'd managed to save the entire ship."

"Alas, m'lady. I do not believe he salvaged more than your Da's—your Dad's floatplan."

They stood in the small room silently for a time.

Then, Laurel asked "What did he say to you, Poseidon... what did he say when he came to you with this...quest?"

Icarus smiled as widely as ever. He cleared his throat and lowered the tone of his voice trying to imitate the depth of Paul's rumbling timbre "*Upon my death you shall be my courier in this matter, delivering to my beloved a small beacon of hope for the darkness which lies ahead.* But his voice is much deeper and it has that catchy accent like m'Da's and Athena and Apollo oh and definitely Hermes I'd go as far as to say Hera but she's been a bit absent lately not to mention the whole business with the Z-man—not sure about his accent though...."

"Stop. Just...do you think he's dead?"

Icarus bit his lower lip.

"Icarus? Do you know if he's alive?"

The boy spoke carefully: "If by him you mean Poseidon,that I do not know. If by him

you mean Paul, I am not qualified to make that distinction. But I trust him. I believe in what he and the brother-gods are trying to do for Olympos."

Laurel stared at the book, wanting to feel the weight of it in her hand again. She wanted to smell the pages, trace her father's hand-writing. "What are they trying to do?"

"Fix their mistake." Icarus put a tentative hand on her shoulder. "I'm afraid I can't be of much help to you in these matters. I can see in your face that there's a thousand questions kept behind that dam of bewilderment. I envy you, really."

"Me? I'm just an Earthsider." She sat beside the float-plan and picked it up carefully.

"That's what I mean. You are an *Earthsider*. You are the first here in millennia, and that means the gods stayed true to their word."

"I suppose that means I'm your only hope? Not a whole lot here to put that much faith in, I'm afraid." She thumbed the pages without opening the book. This was her ritual. The book felt real. Its leather cover still supple though cracked and worn by decades of being shoved into a back pocket.

"We've been at war ever since Earthsiders and Olympos parted ways." Icarus sighed heavily but Laurel was only half listening to him.

The book's binding remained firm, and overall it didn't

show a single spec of evidence that it had been at the bottom of the Mediterranean Sea for a year. Laurel eased the pages open gently, catching a glimpse of her father's halting printed-cursive. She smiled with relief. "The writing is still intact."

"I'm glad for you, m'lady." Icarus stepped away from her though she hardly noticed as she skimmed through the pages expecting no more surprises. She'd read through her father's journal a thousand times before losing *The Ghost*. If Paul had it, why keep it from her? If he could retrieve the float plan from *The Ghost* why didn't he raise the entire ship to the surface? Her stomach tightened and turned thinking about it. The taint from Mathropos had quieted, the fluttering thought silent.

She flipped backward through the pages and stopped in the center at a peculiar symbol which appeared to be branded into the paper. This was new, something from Paul.

In the center, it appeared to be the symbol for pi. To the right of that, an ankh or a half-moon atop a cross? Below the pi symbol sat a ragged, broken capital E. It was more than that, she knew but didn't yet have the whole picture. But the symbol looked as if it belonged on the page, as if her father had burned it into the paper at the same time he had penciled plans for redecking *The Ghost*. She flipped through the rest of the pages searching for another occurrence but stopped when she saw Paul's handwriting: *My lighthouse,* it began.

Immediately thin tears poured from her eyes. She let them fall, despite her earlier admonishment not to weep. Except for the salutation, Paul's normally elaborate handwriting appeared stilted, perhaps even reserved...maybe he was attempting to mimic Dad's handwriting? For that reason she would have missed his note had he not written the L of lighthouse in the same way he penned her name.

"I will take my leave of you, Laurel. When you're ready, come topside." he paused as if to say more. Instead he gave her a brief hug and left her alone.

Laurel's left hand held the journal, her right caressed the owl's head pendant while she read Paul's message out loud.

My lighthouse,

I can see you, sitting in the cabin of Trutina's Balance, holding this journal and hating me for dying, for hiding this most precious memento from you. Your delicate hands clutching at the owl's head, perhaps there are tears in your eyes, and if not they are shimmering and full, too stubborn to fall. There are no words I can write that will heal your heart. I would that I could reach through the ink of these letters and once more taste the salt of your skin.

All I can do is ask for your faith in our love and patience with the tasks ahead of you. I dare not write more else those who oppose us will surely set to ruin the tenuous architecture my brothers and I have painstakingly built these last several months.

Even now as I write this while you sleep beside me, I can feel the Allagi beginning; the Etherium calls me too soon I think for I want only to lay beside you, pull you close and forget. I think now that is the most wonderful gift you have given me, Laurie—allowing me to love you as a man *and granting me a brief respite from being a god...a reprieve I have wandered through an eternity to find.*

Already, I miss you and we have not yet parted. I love you, my Lighthouse.

Find me, Laurie...find me.

TWENTY-FIVE

He did not sleep.

He was not awake.

Death must be sitting upon my back, holding me in the black waters until I succumb.

Part of him gladly would do so to end the torment brought upon him by the storms raging all around. But he knew storms well, had weathered more than a fair share in his lifetime. Always will their destruction provide the means for fresh growth, and always in their wake some sadness remains. Such was the price he paid to be the god of oceans.

In the blackness, he felt nothing but he knew he was cold. Chilled to the edge of being frozen. He could not move his arms or legs, dared not turn his head lest that set off another storm. He had managed to gauge the troughs and crests of this sea well-enough to know he would not stay afloat much longer.

And that part of him that was ready to succumb sighed at the thought of just letting the sea consume him. How glorious would that be? To become the waters of the ocean— to fully merge with *Thalassa* and glide along currents to wherever they may take you? He allowed himself to reach out, to feel the edge of that current. He knew, if he wished it, *Thalassa* would embrace him and return him to his origins. But before going further, he felt *her* reaching back toward him.

His beloved.

She hovered just outside the drafts and eddies, whirling within the storm, tethered to him by a fiber of light so thin his breath could snap the connection.

She is a trick brought by the storms, the eagerness whispered in the blackness.

He considered the possibility, for within a storm of any magnitude there are mirages and illusions to trick the most accomplished seaman.

Turn from her or the storm will consume you, drag you to her depths and leave you rotting at the bottom!

He tensed for a jolt but none came. There was only the darkness, and then a thin light from a great distance, probing through that darkness in search of him.

Hide! The eagerness cajoled him. *Hide or she will pull you out of the darkness and the storms will see you and sink you! Ask to be one with the Oceans, with Thalassa, and it shall be so.*

But he did not hide. He waited. Sometimes, storms broke without warning. Sometimes, cutting to port or starboard put you right in the path of a new storm. Sometimes, being adrift was the only option you had to stay afloat.

The light came to him gracefully but spirited. In the light, he saw his beloved's face shadowed and murky and indistinct. But he knew her because he had felt her before. This time, however, it was stronger though not any closer.

You hover in the eye and you will drown! You will drown! You will DROWN!

The eagerness rattled him, tried to force him to react but before it only wanted him to succumb to the blackness now it seemed frightened. He wanted to fight it, he wanted to rip from the moorings of this dock and swim free.

The light traced along his body, though he could not move to see it and he could not be sure he still had a body. He knew it as he knew storms and oceans that the light had come to help him.

It was in his bones.

He opened himself to it and allowed what was left of himself to be invaded by the light. And suddenly, he knew *everything*.

His eyes peeled open showing him the clear pool of water over which the Fates had suspended him. His body burned in agony from their torture. His own Threads ripped out of his core to keep him prisoner. The regrets, fears, and condemnation of others' Threads corrupting his will....

Or so they thought.

He had but seconds to tell her before the Fates would descend upon him to return him to the blackness.

Poseidon took hold of his Threads, though the raging fire-wall of pain threatened to do what the Fates had, so far, only toyed with, and brought himself upright. Perpendicular to the ceiling, he heaved with the remaining ounces of his strength and drew closer to the scarce drops of water that had collected above him.

He needed but one.

TWENTY-SIX

Laurel lay beside her father's journal for a long time after Icarus left; the symbol forgotten, Paul's letter warming her.

She cried again, just a little, rereading Paul's words. Her heart had suspended her growing aggravation over being lied to. Paul had his reasons and surely seeing this through to the end would make all of that worth it. *He still has some explaining to do...if Paul is alive.* She sealed the doubt away. As her dad always said, *There is no chart to navigate any man's heart, and th'Lord knows his shoals and currents change more often than those in th' Diamond.*

Dad was here now.

He had heard her calling out to the heavens last night and he'd found some way to get her the floatplan; through Poseidon or not, Dad had had his hands in this.

And she wept quietly again as she roamed through the floatplan, reminiscing. Dad kept his nautical life in these pages from charts to equipment lists full of items necessary to complete the journey to Greece. He also sketched and wrote poetry and it was these last that made Laurel most sad...most happy to read them again.

Until after the funeral, she had had no idea her father possessed such skills. Rough, bold, even startling, the poetry revealed a man with a broken heart long covered in the barnacles of life. She found her favorite, *Bones*, and read it out loud, imagining her father's cracked voice speaking to her from the pages:

Beneath her skin
the bones of her mothers' before her
talk in pictures
of places she will never visit.

The pictures travel
through her heart
in the blood of her fathers' before her
singing songs with words she will never speak.

The words become children
Made of old bones and old blood
Made of forgotten pictures and songs
With her heart
Beating.
Beating.
Beating.

BENEATH THE POEM her father had written himself a note: "Lil fin's bday tomorrow!". She had no idea to which birthday he referred, he did not date the poem but she guessed it was within her last two because it was the final poem he'd written in the floatplan.

Laurel closed the book, swung her feet over the edge of the cot and stretched a million worries out of her back. Her hands came to rest on the pendant and waited for any sign of whatever magic Paul used to reach her.

None came.

I'm right here, she tried to force the thought through the pendant in the same way she'd tried to reach her father the other night.

Nothing.

"It's okay. I know you're there somehow...in some way." She stood up and decided this was her life. This improbable, remarkable, wonderful and unknown mythos wasn't a dream and it wasn't going away. "Different rules, different waters, same bones right dad?.

Foreign ports are like that, he'd explained to her after one of fifty different times they'd moved from one Coast Guard station to another. *Shanghai, Tripoli, New York, it don't matter th'port...the storms'll come as they'll come even if you've lost yer bearings. You'll know what needs doin—that sense is in yer bones—and yer bones go wherever you go, lil'fin.*

Trust your bones.

The taint from Mathropos now lay dormant. The fluttering thought which may or may not be from Paul had settled somewhere distant. But she knew there was a battle to come.

Laurel promised herself from now on she would listen to her bones more closely. And the first thing she heard her bones saying was what Paul had been trying to tell her—what she'd suddenly become so enraged about during her flight with Icarus—that Paul was alive. *I'll find you, I promise.* And if that means swimming to Athena, to Ares, to Aphrodite, even digging down to the Underworld to have a tussle with Hades, well then that would be...that would be the stretch of it.

She slid the floatplan-journal beneath her pillow, and smoothed the covers. She undid all of Icky's adjustments, popped the brass fasteners and slipped out of her pelpos. She searched through the drawers of the dresser and found clothing more suitable for work aboard a ketch: khaki trousers and a brown t-shirt. She splashed her face in cold water, fluffed her hair and left her cabin.

Once topside, Laurel made a direct line to the pilot house where Trutina still stood, his brown taut-skinned arms working the helm the way an artist might a brush. It occurred to her that all the while she'd been fighting her own demons. The Angler had maintained the course of *The Balance* toward Athena's island. She suspected it was at some cost, otherwise the man's convictions would not have shown themselves with such fierceness earlier.

Rumbles of thunder several leagues to the southwest caught her attention briefly; the intensity of the storm didn't appear to have worsened. *That's the thing about storms,* she set her father's voice aside and focused on repairing the damage she'd done to her relationship with Trutina. *Be buoyant,* she pleaded with herself. *Stay your course,* she repeated the order over and over.

Laurel chose her first words carefully: "I didn't know, Trutina."

Sunlight fell across the water all around *The Balance*, making pools of golden auras, which the ship's prow punctured and dissipated without a second thought. The gentle hand of a steady breeze at least four knots strong pushed *The Balance* along to their destination. Wispy white veins meandered toward fat cauliflower-shaped clouds, probably the precursor of another storm—perhaps an ancestor of the one she'd seen with Icarus earlier.

Trutina's stance did not change.

Laurel refused to leave until this thing between them had been settled.

The persistent *kussshh* of *The Balance* cutting through the Olympian waters became the only dialogue between them.

She gave the owl's head a playful tug, closed her eyes as the wind and spray played over her face and through her hair. A minute passed and Trutina yet remained silent. Opening her eyes she set herself to make things right again.

"I've been alone for a long time too," she started, taking a small step to place herself in line with Trutina. "My mother died when I was three; I remember the idea of her more than anything physical. Mostly sounds and sensations. I have photos of us, but those memories are Kodak moments not mine." She watched him for some sign of emotion or even acknowledgement of her presence. Detecting none she pushed on, unabated. "Last year, my father died suddenly. He was a lot like you, a man of the sea. He was a Coastie almost all of his adult life. If he wasn't out at sea, he was walking her shores and if he couldn't do that he was talking about the ocean.

"When he died, I thought I could handle it. I did, for a while, I guess. But there was no one left for me to check on and no one left to check on me. So I did the only sensible thing I've ever done: I disappeared. I secluded myself. I drank. A lot. Too much, truth be told. And then I left my home altogether."

The man remained a salty statue of silence. She didn't care, it felt good to put the events of the last year into order and out loud.

"I sank my dad's ship, figured I was about to die and then you found me. 'Course I didn't know you then. I didn't know *any* of this then. But I'm getting better now. Thanks to Icarus and you." She dared to put a hand on his shoulder and was relieved when Trutina didn't flinch or pull away. The blooming thing left by the Keeper remained in check, the moth tacit.

She decided to try one last thing, something that always worked with Dad. Men of the sea think like the sea. "I am really sorry about what I said to you, Trutina. Most of me is knotted up inside—like a Carrick Bend but I can't find the standing or bitter end so I'm at a loss. And until I can make sense of the knots, I can't promise I'm going to be myself."

Trutina dropped his hands from the helm and turned to face her. His white eyes glistened prominently, showing a crispness that gave the impression he might actually see her. His cracked lips, however, remained desperately in need of Chapstick. She counted a dozen small scars across his face and twice that on his arms and hands, though none of them could rival the brutal ghost of a wound that ran from clavicle to beltline.

"Isa knew knots well. Her hands, small as yours, could tie off a line faster than any man. She would tell you the only way to deal with a knot tied by another man's hand is to cut off his hand to keep him from doing it again." His chuckle came in huffing rasps.

Laurel smiled and tried to picture the woman who had loved this man.

"Poseidon chose well," Trutina continued. "You have the salt of the ocean in your eyes. Isa would have enjoyed your spirit upon this ship." The old man sighed and turned his face to the gathering clouds, his face darkening. "I am sorry for my ill treatment of you. Since Isa's absence, I have neglected my own knots. Though it is a poor excuse; the war has left me unaccustomed to ferrying any but the rare Olympian-born and even then they grace my deck with silence."

"I think it's safe to say neither of us has had our hands securely on the rudder." She took his hand in hers.

He clasped hers firmly, shook it once and said, "Spoken like the daughter of a seaman. Our hull is whole again. Come, I wish to show you something."

Trutina did not wait, turning away from her and heading back into the pilot house. He caressed a dark globe of glass hanging overhead and brought it to glowing green life with two passes of his hand. Thunder rumbled distantly, rolling back and forth among the clouds like a wayward barrel half-full of irons. "The Fates?" she asked pointing toward the source.

The Angler did not answer, instead guided her attention to a draftsman's table upon which lay an elegant chart. Wide fat scrolling letters along the bottom proclaimed its contents to be the *Αρχιπέλαγος Ólimbos*, the Archipelagos of Olympos. Laurel admired the scrolling spread of islands, immediately identifying Paul's island in the southwestern-most corner of the chart. She also saw the jagged strip of the Reef: here a charcoal-black thumb-wide stain running north-south, edge to edge. Among all the islands, however, she could not find the one thing she was sure should be there. "This isn't right."

The old Angler cocked his head in that bird-like manner.

"There's something missing from this chart."

Trutina studied her and the horizon at the same time; it was difficult to tell if he was even awake sometimes, she decided. She needed to ask him what exactly he did see.

"The Olympian gods are supposed to live on Mount Olympos."

"Icarus!" a moment after he barked the boy's name, his head popped in, upside down, from the pilothouse overhead.

"You barged...bargained...bellowed...below...bellll...bell-oh? The diction is running rampant and I've naught an instrument to capture it." Icky, presumably perched above, disappeared for a moment, made a series of cantankerous movements out of sight and finally swooped down into the pilothouse. He primped himself carefully, smoothing mostly air out of his impossibly wrinkled shirt, finally taking his place at the table elbows firmly planted.

"You have been out of the eye of your father too long." Trutina moved Laurel closer to the table placing his hand in the small of her back.

Trust your bones girl, her father's voice reverberated strongly through her, emanating from the Angler's touch. "I know it's a nautical chart; it's not really that much different than an Earthsider one and though my Greek's a little rusty, I can make out most of these names. I'm guessing one island for each god but what I don't understand is why Mount Olympos isn't shown? Earthsider mythology puts the twelve Olympians all living together in a grand mansion atop Mount Olympos."

The two of them stared at her, Icarus more quizzically; Trutina just the same white-eyed ubiquitous glare.

Icarus' grin spread slowly. "I'll take this one Trutina," although the old man had made no attempt at answering. Laurel smiled as Icarus began his show.

"From a time before the gods of Olympos—" mock deep voice, lots of unnecessary gestures.

"Boy, the storms are nigh—thar be no time for your

theatrics." Trutina leveled at him with a stoic, impenetrable glare.

"Right. But I didn't rehearse the short version so..." Icarus' wings began to expand.

The old man did not turn as he spoke to her. "Th'gods have their secrets, girl. This be one." Trutina still kept an eye on the ocean ahead. "We and you have not th'time to tarry. Th'storms draw close—"

"That's the thing about storms, isn't it? Sometimes they break without warning and sometimes being adrift is the only option you have to stay afloat." Laurel felt Paul all around and through her so strongly, so suddenly as to be nearly over-whelming. The words she'd spoken had not come from her thoughts.

The boy and Angler did not seem to notice.

Icarus added, "Storms can shake your banes...brains? Bones! Aye! So I'm guessing that whatever you did to upset the triumvirate of happiness whom we all know and love as the Sisters of Fate must have been quite high on their 'I hope *this* never happens or else we'll create an all-consuming storm that threatens the fabric of Olympos' list."

Trutina's face did not change but his glare was enough to get the boy back on track.

He cleared his throat and continued his explanation: "Olympos has always been a collection of islands, Laurel. The Greeks—specifically a chap named Homer—crafted the idea of a lofty perch for the Z-man and the rest of the goddies. I guess, Earthsiders just have a nifty way of forcing the truth to fit what they *see* instead of what they *feel*. Da told me that you'll find a lot of your myths mistaken...nay mislabeled?...misplaced. Aye. But wait til you see our version of the Parthenon on the Z-man's island." Icarus framed the upper right quadrant of the chart using both hands, emphasizing its importance with a long, slow whistle.

"Theatrics," Trutina pointed off to the starboard side of *The Balance* but Laurel only saw the diminishing glimmer of the setting sun.

She rolled the pendant between her fingers, her skin felt tight, her scalp damp. Heaviness crept into her shoulders, pulling them back. Her eyes burned as if from allergies and she felt that same edginess returning but with a vengeance. "Are you pointing toward Athena's island or up at the damn sky? Why are you standing so close to me? Can't either of you just answer my questions? *Borite na me voitheisete!*?" Laurel slapped her hands on the chart hard enough to shake the table.

Icarus paled, Trutina kept his position.

"I need some...I need...I just need *water...*" tiny pricks of electrical energy stabbed into her finger tips through the pendant. She closed her eyes and felt like she was falling sideways. When she spoke again the words were not her own. "***Keep yer prow west of the Deucalion current, Angler...comes soon the surge...I need but one***."

"She speaks in the tongue of the gods'?" Trutina's voice tightened as he stepped protectively toward Laurel.

Icarus flanked her right side taking her arm gently.

The bloom expanded pushing fiery memories of her father's death into every crevice of her mind. The fluttering thought, she knew now was a tenuous and gossamer connection to Paul, struggled to stay aloft. "Icky...something's happening to me...." She did not feel dizzy, exactly, just drifting. "I think it's—" her body seized up suddenly, arms locked at the elbow, knees rock solid and immobile. She looked at her fingers splayed over the islands, felt them aching to crawl across the chart.

"Trutina, what do we do?" Icarus' voice cracked with panic.

The Angler brought his hands up to Laurel's face.

"*Stamatíste*! *Afisé me ísihi*!" Laurel swatted his hands away. "*Signomi, ala then milao elinika.*, I can't stop...it...can't...stop...*estanome kala.*" She stopped fighting whatever held her and immediately her hands drifted like a planchette over the islands desperately seeking something.

"The storms call to her." Trutina left them abruptly to take control of *The Balance*. Fat, ominous cumulonimbus clouds billowed upward overhead. Thick cloud-tendrils spiraled away from it like smoky vines. Lightning coruscated through the base of the clouds, tongues of blue light flickering between the tendrils against the cobalt of the twilight ocean sky.

"I can feel them, Icar...Icky. The Fates are close—please don't let them come...Please don't let them hurt me again!" She was not looking at the deck of *The Balance*. Instead, she saw a cold mausoleum but she was not at ground level...she was...*floating*? No. She was hangning... her position showed her a view from the ceiling down, her blood falling into the pool below spreading out in elegant Rorschach patterns.

Trutina grunted with effort to maintain an even keel.

"We need to move Trutina! We cannot let her be taken by the Fates!"

"*The Balance* moves, boy! Thar be no more to draw from her!"

"You lie, Angler!" Icarus' words came fiercely, turning Laurel's head to make sure it was still him.

Lighting zig-zagged between clouds, a few blue tongues

came near to touching the waters. Laurel felt herself returning to normal, felt the connection to Paul rapidly unraveling, the taint of the Fates also receding but begrudgingly. She wanted to take up the pendant and crush it into her palm hard enough to bring blood but her hands fumbled over the chart, a few fingers tracing the north-easterly path of the Deucalion Current, her fingers frantic pace finally slowing as they reached Anaktoro.

"You can barely fly a league, boy, let alone pilot a ship. Do not question me again." Trutina's words came icily.

Laurel did not resist but the more open she allowed herself to become in an effort to keep the connection to Paul, the more tumultuous the storms—those overhead and aboard ship between the boy and the Angler. Whatever power worked to bring her Paul's presence must also be the same that drew the Fates.

She would not give in until she knew what he meant for her to see, damn the Fates.

"You *know* my meaning, Angler. Da built *The Balance* for you **and** Isoropia; you don't need her to—"

Trutina turned from the helm, grabbed Icarus and thrust him against the wall, shuddering the pilothouse. "Still your tongue, child. My hands bled to build *The Balance*, not your father's! I gave Daedalus the specifications down to the weight of the brass nails securing her hull. But na'er again will you—"

Icarus pulled out and away from Trutina's grip in a white blur. He spun behind the Angler and put one arm against the back of Trutina's head and with the other he locked the old man's hands in the small of his back. "Either use this ship as it was meant to be or I will fly her there myself!"

"You would not betray me so, boy!"

"I would for her sake!"

"Think boy, this be the witchery of the Fates." Trutina did not sound entirely convinced himself.

"Does not your precious *Balance* bear the tattoo on her deck as a reminder of your indiscretions? Is that not the reason your beloved was Removed?" Icarus' face had become a rictus of anguish.

Trutina wrenched himself from Icarus' grip and brought an elbow crashing down between his wings. "Athena's isle be too far to fly on your crepe-paper wings!"

Icarus crumpled beneath the blow, but growled out "Would you let the Earthsider be Removed *too*, then?" tears rolled down his face.

"Stop," Laurel rasped. The storm boiled around them. She knew that if she held on to the connection any longer, more than scars would be left among them.

"Move the ship as she was *meant* to be moved, Trutina. Please." Icarus pleaded.

Trutina bowed his head.

An electric moment passed wherein something changed which Laurel could not quite put her finger on.

She watched Trutina, expecting for him to glow, levitate, or radiate some ethereal luminance. But instead, nothing happened.

Physically, he did not touch the ship's helm and yet *The Balance* moved as if he had. Steadily, she rose up on the waters despite the chaos of the storm, lurching forward as if propelled on a triple set of 8ohp engines. The prow crashed against the surface, her wake a razor through the waves. Trutina now controlled *The Balance* by will alone and though she seemed to respond sluggishly at first, she now moved eight times faster than before.

Trutina brought his head up to face Laurel and he was beautiful. His eyes had shed the white cataracts and now shimmered a delicate green like the glow orbs around the deck. His face burned golden but his neck and body shuddered as if he were in pain. And when he sang, his words resonated an ache so deep Laurel thought the storms shied back in fear of being stung by his grief.

The Balance cleared the storms within a minutes, surging through the ocean on the power of Trutina's will alone.

Remember the dream, Laurie...find me.

Paul's voice washed through her as cool and serene as an early spring shower and then the bond simply left her.

Behind them, the storms dissolved and the darkness among them ebbed away with the last few strikes of lighting.

Icarus caught her before she hit the deck, pulling her close and covering her with his wings. "I will see you safe again into the arms of your beloved," he whispered gently.

Laurel faded into unconsciousness, Trutina's aching song guiding her to sleep.

TWENTY-SEVEN

Poseidon let go of the bond, blood raining from his eyes and mouth staining the pool below, a whisper of a smile staining his face.

But he would die here now, that much was assured. *Every small gesture she ever made remains etched upon my thoughts, every shade of every black curl forever entangled in my hands, every touch upon my skin are now gentle ghosts playing upon my own.*

He feared death and this surprised him because, before Laurie, he knew he could face Thanatus eye to eye and walk in his footsteps to Tartarus. Now, the grey death monger will have to pierce me with my own trident and drag me down fighting before I walk in his footsteps.

He missed Laurie deeply...more than he missed the swell of the seas and the currents of the oceans. She had entered him body and soul in a way no woman ever had before her. And no event after her could ever match. He was hers stem to stern.

The great hall hummed with heavy silence and throbbed with darkness. He knew The Keeper would soon return, she would read his Threads and she would terrorize him for what he'd done. If she could find it, that was. He had learned, too late, how to redirect Mathropos, how to create mirages within his pattern. Makaisi was even more easily duped. Mira, however, he feared her more than the other two not because of what she'd done to him but what he still did not know about her.

He had stopped bleeding now, his breathing leveling out, his eyesight not as blurry though his head still rung with pain and not entirely his own. The Angler would never forgive him the damage done but debts were meant to be paid, their consequences enforced. And it had been for her, after all.

He felt frail and vulnerable, though not to the credit of his current circumstances. Hanging from the ceiling by his own Threads brought endless torment, but it was reaching out to Laurie that truncated his life-force by hundreds of years. He knew she'd seen through his eyes, likely felt his torment; such was the penance of being a messenger. What he'd not been prepared for was feeling her doubt made buoyant by slivers of regret and the floatsam and jetsam of her old demons. *I'm sorry, Laurie...I'm sorry for buffering my world, for hiding the truth, for being dishonest.* And he'd felt something else in there...a doubled-headed thing. One constructed, one experienced. The constructed thing would tumble soon but the other? Thought dormant and discarded, he knew the event was so traumatizing she'd buried it beneath a mountain of guilt. *I have tread where no man ought to...please forgive me Laurie.*

Except she'd never know his regret for the lies or his remorse for awakening what she'd tried to keep in hibernation because, before she reached Anaktoro, he would be dead.

Truly dead, not merely transitioning from one perception

to another. If this had worked, if he could have completed what he and his brothers had schemed millennia ago.... Even now the Changed—the Allagi—tugged at him, eager to shift him from Olympos to Earthside and renew the Balance wrought by Gaia and Uranus through their union. *I will not live to see you again, my beautiful Earthsider. I will not live to walk the Outer Banks with you and listen to your stories of sandcastles and regattas.*

He realized he had begun to weep and was surprised for the second time in twenty minutes as the tears were genuine. In truth, he had not failed Olympos, only his beloved. Zeus and Hades would see his death avenged, their plans completed—that had been their pact from the beginning.

Poseidon relaxed then. What is done be done, what be lost be forgotten, what can be kept cherished. His father had taught him that much. He would not, however, go down without a fight....something else his father had taught him in battle and in life. *You can bend and break like the dry reed or you can bend and strike back as the supple yew.* He drew a long, slow breath tasting the moisture in the air and relishing it like ambrosia.

He smiled thinly and spoke aloud so that even if he were unconscious, Mathropos would still find his words caught within his Threads. "Come to me, Keeper. I have a bone to pick with you."

TWENTY-EIGHT

"Drink, girl." The voice warmed her bones.

"Dad?" she smiled broadly, reaching out for him anxious to feel the permanent stubble of his white whiskers drawn against hers, abrading her face.

"Drink, m'lady." The voice changed to a boy's and Laurel peeled open her eyes.

Amorphous multi-colored shapes hovered around her. Some green, one red or maroon, another an angry brown. She closed her eyes again and pulled her legs up to her chest. This had happened before; dreams of Dad haunting her, reminding her of how she'd failed him. She had drifted away from him and from the ocean and he never let her forget that. "Go away!" she pouted and slapped at the air to keep the dreams from getting inside and worsening the throbbing hum in her skull.

"Their touch remains," her Dad's words scolded.

"I'm sorry," she whimpered, feeling for the blanket, that gray fleece one he'd given her in 2000—you know the one with the blue silkscreened Coast Guard emblem? I always sleep with that one after a long night out.

A hangover, you mean?

Okay, fine—a hangover.

Yeah you drank a lot after Dad died.

It kept the waves away so shut up, shut up!

"Laurel, you need to drink this or it's going to get worse." The boy again—who the hell was he? A new spirit to torment her in her dreams. "Piss off," she slurred the words into *pizzof* and that made her giggle. "I am *not* as drunk as you *think* I am!" she laughed again and her body hurt more.

"I think her mind's been hornswaggled...hijacked, aye! Hijacked—what spirits of the sea can work witchery such as this?"

"No spirits boy. The Sisters three have tampered once too often with her threads. This and I have danced together before." Her Dad's voice wavered in a funny way. Familiar but not Dad-familiar. Familiar because—

Because it's better to drift than have a course to run?

Shut the hell up! God you're annoying.

That's the pot calling the kettle black!

"Laurel, it is I, Icarus. Sometimes Icky. I'm going to have to open your mouth again—please don't bite me this time?" the boy's voice sounded familiar too.

Her Dad laughed. "What's so funny, Dad?" she asked peeling open her eyes again. She could see a pair of faces peering back at her their heads illuminated by green orbs of light floating around them. Wait. The lights weren't floating, she was. No, that wasn't true either. They were all floating, moving like they were on a ship.

Laurel's awareness rushed back in suddenly and she reconnected with the consciousness she'd had before everything went to hell: "They're here, Mira and Makaisi are here —they're in the sky!"

Icky glanced overhead, raising his wings. "I thought I smelled something foul."

"Quiet your theatrics, boy. For now." Trutina slid past Icarus to ease Laurel up to a sitting position, his coarse hands cradling her head, his voice as soft as she'd ever heard him. "Trust the salt of your bones, Laurel."

Laurel sat shaken, hearing her father's words from Trutina's mouth.

"I did not know your father but I count him among my brothers of the sea. I am, however, not him though I trust you will not hate me for using his words to settle you."

"I do not...I cannot hate you, Trutina. I am sorry I've brought this upon you. Upon both of you." Laurel wiped her face with both hands, pulling black strands of curled locks out of her mouth. "I'm sorry, for everything."

"Well, you did ruffle my feathers. And I think you might have scratched the railing there a bit, but all in all I suppose we can manage to forgive you." Icarus knelt beside her where she lay on the deck.

"What happened? I remember seeing Mira in the storm...or did I? And you two were having a knock down drag out fight about...about..." *Paul was here; I felt him all over me. I can still smell him.* The fluttering thought was surely him.

She toyed with the pendant, recollecting.

"Aye, the Fates leaned heavy upon us but their witchery have we eluded for a short while. Still, we best not drift here long; the isle of Athena be but a few leagues ahead." Trutina pressed Laurel's shoulder then stood and went about his ministrations to *The Balance*.

"You two fought. Because of me," she said, still processing last night and the fact that they were almost upon

Athena's island. "How did we cover so much ocean...oh...yeah...you coerced Trutina into super-charging the ship."

"If need be I would have paddled my feet to save you." Icarus blushed as he turned away.

"Thank you, Icky." She felt love for the boy; his heart too big for his own chest, his mind full of whatever Earthsider-myths Olympians told their children. "Again, I am sorry I brought all of this upon you both."

"Please, m'lady, do not apologize for the twisted trio. All of us have suffered their diabolical machinations at one time or another." He helped her stand and before the silence became too heavy added: "You really must drink this before too long, m'lady." He held a rough-hewn bowl half-full of a dirty liquid in which floated bits of what looked like bark.

"You're joking." But Icarus held it to her without further jest.

"Well, what's it supposed to do?" Laurel tentatively took the bowl from the boy, smelled the liquid and arched her eyebrows. "Hey, it smells like...pot!? Is this marijuana?"

"I know not your meaning of smelling like a pot. This is sage tea. It will aid in the mending of your ragged threads." Trutina offered as he swept past them carrying rope, disappearing behind the mizzen as he reached the aft.

"Hunh. A year ago I'd have tossed this overboard and called you both crazy right before I followed it." She tested the beverage and found it tepid. "Show me Vegas," she muttered and drank the concoction. "Oh my—*ghack*! It's got a bit of a kick."

"That would be the ginger. Or it could be the dendroli-vano. I should warn you that you'll probably feel a little woozy for a while. That tends to be the primary side effect as your Threads settle." Icarus took the bowl from her and pulled her to her feet.

"The touch of the Fates recedes," she whispered.

"Aye, m'lady, and before long you shall be all yourself... all of yourself? You shall be your whole self!" he smiled widely, his brown eyes glittering with gold in the morning sunlight.

"I think I need to lie down, Icky." She started forward, staggered, caught herself and then allowed Icarus to assist her.

"Let us to your cabin then!"

"Easy, not too fast." She wrapped her left arm in his as they walked.

"Do you remember speaking the language of the gods last night?"

"No. In fact, I remember very little. Blotches of things, shapes and colors mostly."

"Well, for an Earthsider, you speak it very well." He paused with her at the steps descending below decks. "Would you like for me to carry you down?"

"No, this I can manage." She took the first step tentatively, felt stable enough, and continued downward. "I remember saying words that didn't belong to me." Her head pounded with dull pain, old memories thundering distantly.

"You said," Icarus cleared his throat and put on his best impression of her southern lilt: *"Keep yer prow west of the Deucalion current, Angler...comes soon the surge...I need but one.* I think you even managed to surprise Trutina."

"Hmm...I spoke in a different language?" They reached the bottom of the steps and suddenly Laurel felt dizziness sweep through her. She braced herself against the wall. "I'm okay," she said to assuage the look of concern on the boy's face. "Just a little dizzy."

"It is good then that you'll take rest soon. And, aye, you spoke the language of the gods. A few Olympians can understand it like Trutina, Da, and myself. But it is rare for a mortal to be able to speak it. Perhaps rarer still that for an Earthsider. Did Posi teach you?"

"No. But I have a feeling he's responsible for it just the same. What do you think I meant by 'I need but one'?"

"Hard to say; you weren't yourself that is for certain." Concern shadowed the boy's face.

"I'll be okay, Icky. All kinds of change happening inside here," she gestured over her body from head to toe. "I think I'll be my whole self, soon enough."

They walked in silence the short distance to Laurel's cabin. Something still bothered her about last night and she knew that in order for her to rest completely she had to ask the boy the truth. "Trutina. He's..."

"Carved from the hardest salt known to mortals?"

"True. But, I have to ask you something about last night. It's the clearest thing I remember...you and Trutina..." she suddenly found it difficult to talk about it, remember them at each other's throats and knowing she caused it.

Icarus chuckled, but there was an underlying tension to it. "He's like m'Da: if you want to encourage an angry bull you sometimes have to be an angrier bull."

"There's something between him and Poseidon, isn't there?" she said it without thinking.

Icarus stayed silent a few moments before answering. "There's a lot I should...well, let me put it this way: As m'Da explains it those two have a history like the Labyrinth. Every corner is duty, every narrow passage is honor. Neither one of them will help the other because if they did, they'd finally be free of it and then...then what would they do, eh?"

Laurel stared at the boy. He wasn't lying, she was certain of that, but he wasn't being entirely forthcoming either. She was really too tired to go on much longer, already she could feel her body sagging into itself. She decided not to pursue what she saw in his eyes and instead said "I only know the Earthsider version of your father, Icky, but already I like yours better. I hope I get to meet him someday."

"I too hope for the same. I believe he would like you. If you'll allow me to get the door for you m'lady" he opened it with a regal flourish. "Welcome to your royal chambers! A comfy bed in a closet."

Laurel crossed the threshold, feeling every joint aching for rest. As she sat on her bed, another blotch from last night coalesced into a solid image. "Icky, Icarus," she could not help herself now, "did Poseidon help Trutina move the *Balance* closer to Athena's island?"

Icarus stretched his wings wide as he yawned and leaned against the door frame. "Zeus' lightning no! That's all the Angler's doing."

"Trutina can will the ship to move faster? Then why didn't he do that from the very beginning? Would have saved all of us a lot of time."

He seemed to be churning over his thoughts before he finally answered. "The stretch of it is, Trutina and this ship are...very well acquainted. He and Isoropia—" Icarus broke off.

Immediately, Laurel felt warmth spill into her from the pendant dangling against her sternum. Paul's voice oscillated around her thoughts and brought a sliver of awareness to Laurel which she could not help but speak aloud. "He lost her and lost his way; Trutina's gift was their love, this ship the force that carried them; they danced upon the whispers of Aeolus..." there was more, she thought, but the warmth faded and the words fluttered away with sensation of Paul.

Silence entered the room for a time but it did not feel

awkward and neither of them made much of an effort to break it.

Finally, Icarus stepped into the cabin, drew water from the tap, filling a bronze cup. He downed the contents quickly, refilled the glass and offered it to Laurel, asking "Topside you...during all that hullabaloo that is...you said you thought you'd never escape the sisters. Do you believe that?" the boy's face darkened.

Laurel regarded him a moment as she sipped from the cup. "Where I come from, fate has become the same thing as luck, chance, consequence, circumstance—people don't attribute their daily mishaps to a trio of bitchy, maniacal old women anymore. Some blame God...most blame themselves. But we aren't caught in their web so deep...I wish I could say with conviction that we'll be free of the Fates, Icky. But I don't really know. "

"Maybe that's the stretch of it then, hm? None of us are free but we don't have to trap ourselves either." He trailed off, examining everything and nothing.

She handed the cup back to Icarus, pulling her knees up and hugging herself tightly. Memories dashed in and out of focus, leaving her again with blotches of color, shapes, and noise. Her life before the island had become the myth and her life here the real one, she thought. She really had struggled with Dad's death. Many demons could be subdued on your way to the bottom of a bottle. And putting together the trip happened as fast as a bolt of lightning, intended to be a salve on her wounds. No, that wasn't the truth. The trip was meant to bring her absolution and forgiveness for her sins. She knew too that the trip had always been her way to make that final attempt at saying she was sorry for not being a better daughter.

"Maybe I need to be alone." Her words came out sharper than she'd intended.

Icarus winced, said "Aye. M'lady." and turned to leave.

"Icarus...Icky, wait. I'm sorry. I didn't it mean it that way. I was really just talking to myself...feeling sorry for myself too. My head and heart and bones are just a mess."

"I understand. After me mum...died...Da and I spent a lot of time piecing the parts back together. He said, when it comes to that sort of puzzle you do what you can with the pieces you've got left. And sometimes you just find the right junk to make new ones." He remained at the doorway.

Laurel said nothing. She felt Paul radiating through the pendant again, though not as strongly. Nor was she entirely sure the sensation came from Paul or the tea. "He loved me, you know. Not in any way I could ever have imagined, either. He remembered things, little elements of Laurel he called them. I don't like crust on my toast and my peanut butter has to be spread all the way to the edge and immediately after the toast pops up. I like my coffee just so...almost a little bit but not too strong; that's how he described it. But he made me laugh, Icky. Oh, I've never met a funnier man, Earthside." She trailed off, drifting really. It hurt more than keeping herself separate from him because the longer she caressed the owl's head, the more memories came drifting up.

"I think I might have made the tea a bit too strong; Da had said to take ease on that particular brew, what with you being an Earthsider and all." Icarus offered her the cup again.

Laurel took it gratefully and emptied it completely this time. "Thank you. That wooziness thing you mentioned is starting to kick in and it's hitting me like a tidal wave." Her eyes fluttered and Paul's presence settled around her.

"I take my leave of you then, m'lady. I believe yon old

Angler could use some companionship, whether he knows it or not."

Laurel wanted to hold on to him, tell him everything was going to be okay. That tomorrow was a new day, and all sorts of other phrases she knew were empty Earthsider platitudes. Instead she squeezed his hand and offered: "A rainy day on the beach is still a day at the beach. That's what my dad used to tell me when he was dragging me out at five a.m. to go fishing."

"I like it. I'll keep that one for later." He turned, stopped, then faced her again looking ready to give her something unexpected and stopped. "I need to tell you that...I am truly sorry for what happened up on deck. Da would have clock-worked a better plan than mine."

"Your plan got us this far, Icky." She stood and brought him into a gentle hug. "Thank you," she whispered into his messy crop of hair.

"For what m'lady? I'm not sure I've alleviated your burdens."

"For being my hero when I didn't have one."

TWENTY-NINE

Icarus stood outside Laurel's cabin until he heard her breathing change from quick and short to long and deep.

He wanted to tell her everything but duty bound him to remain tacit on all but what was necessary. Posi and Da would never forgive him if he told Laurel what she really was. That would be far worse than flying too close to the sun, even with what he'd done to his Da.

But she called me her hero....

I do not know by what magics these gods and fathers conduct their business, but I could use a dose of it now. It would not be easy to continue duping the Earthsider but he knew it would be far worse trying to protect her *after* the truth.

Finally, he smiled and pulled himself away from the door, heading topside. He began to convince himself that what little more he did know would not change anything for the Earthsider. She would still hurt with the missing of Posi. She would still be plagued by what the Fates had done to her until they reached Athena's island, he suspected. And she would still have to complete her journey to Anaktoro. The only difference would be knowing how valuable she was to the why of it all.

He mounted the steps to the top deck, having decided that the best thing he could do for Laurel was to remain by her side through it all. Even if that meant his hero status would be tainted for withholding the truth.

He glided across the deck over the worn mural depicting Posi's battle with the Fates and landed inches from Trutina who made no indication he knew Icarus was there or not.

"You have done well to keep your word to Lord Poseidon. To your father."

How does he do that? "I am not all feathers, Angler." He took a perch on the starboard railing, watching the ocean's fluid face for signs of the Fates.

"Aye. Does she sleep?"

"I think so. Trutina?" The man gave no response. "Do you believe the brother gods will win?"

Winds came from a distance, tousling his hair, ruffling his feathers. He could smell hyacinth and dead fish. Trutina's reply startled him, the man had taken so long in responding.

"It is not our place to gauge wins and losses among the gods, boy. Either way, it is we who bear the burdens of both."

The winds moved on, taking the mixture of sweetness and death with it. Icarus wondered when he would gain the ability to sum up so dire a situation as this war with the Fates as Trutina and his father always seemed able to do.

"Boy, on the 'morrow your wings...be they ready?"

He thought about flexing them fully with a wicked snap to show the Angler indeed, his wings were more than ready. Instead, he brought them in tightly, dropped from his perch and took his place carefully beside Trutina.

The Angler said nothing, only offered him a black handled dirk in a thin animal-skin sheath.

Icarus took it, surprised by the weight of such a slim blade. He extracted the weapon from the sheath and marveled at its double-edged bite. It took him only a moment to secure it to his waist. "Thank you, Trutina."

"Aye. Sometimes serving as a protector requires more mettle than muscle."

Icarus opened his mouth to point out the play on words and then stopped himself. Doing things like that almost always ended in a ruined moment, or so a lot of people told him. Instead, he put his hand over the blade and hoped he could use it with the same wisdom which Trutina had given it to him.

THIRTY

Amynta could not help but weep for the man.

Deidros, a fisherman by trade. He never spoke much except for the rare occasion someone asked his opinion on the gods. Deidros would spit into the sands, kick at it and then pull his soft round head back and erupt with expletives no child should hear before adulthood. Here he floated now: a husk upon a raft. His sixty-year old body looked a day short of one hundred, the skin so taut at his joints and over his skull that Amynta feared his bones would soon split through completely. Deidros' eyes kept their glimmer and that above all sickened her the most.

No. That is not the worst, the worst is that I have to leave him.

Indeed, she had tarried too long already making sure that Oli and Harlan were safe with Ellera; the girl would soon be a mother herself and certainly could use the training. That did not make her departure any easier on her heart. And here she stood now lamenting her own misfortune while poor Deidros idly stroked the shore like human driftwood. The least she could do was anchor him, hope that another fisherman would come along soon and see to his burial rites. First, she patted the bundle beneath her stolla, readjusted it unnecessarily to be sure it would not break with the impending effort and then set to dragging Deidros up on the shore.

Amynta thought of the Earthsider, again and again she weighed her actions with the anticipated benefits. And again she stopped herself because she was not endangering her life and those of her sons for the Earthsider alone. But if the Earthsider had been sent home the day she'd arrived, or better yet if she had simply never come at all then...then.... "Then the war would still be happening, and Vettias would still be dead." She told herself.

She admired Laurel Nash for the love she shared with Lord Poseidon. His happiness had changed the island in ways she was sure even he would never know. Watching them become fall in love was a good ache, she told herself time and time again. It did not lessen the emptiness she felt without Vettias, nor could it replace her love for him, but completing this quest for Lord Poseidon might well keep her, Oli, Harlan, and all of Olympos from joining her husband.

"You may look a pile of dried leaves, poor Deidros, but you weigh half a cow." His eyes continued their unblinking glimmer despite her efforts to shutter them. His lids were thin crusts lodged deeply above each eye. She had seen the handiwork of the Fates before. Too many times before. In the early days of the war, before Vettias sacrificed himself, the Sisters of Fate took many an Olympian as consort, confidant, and candy. Amynta shuddered at the thought: to die witnessing your fate sucked out of your core.

"I shall send word for you, Deidros. You will not be

denied your place in Asphodel." Amynta fetched a pair of coins from her satchel and laid them gently over Deidros' ever-open eyes. "If you see Vettias, tell him I still believe."

She turned to face northeast, peering out across the unforgiving waters and hoped she faced Zeus' mansion directly. "Lord Poseidon, by my oath as your *oikonomos*, this task I shall see through to the end." Again she checked the bundle safely hidden beneath her amber stolla, eager to be free of it. If she was to reach Anaktoro by her master's deadline she could not afford any more delays, self-imposed or otherwise. She kissed her hand and laid it flat to the sands beneath her, "If ever again we kiss, my love." Amynta left Deidros and continued away from the second lighthouse, her task there finally complete. She hoped Lord Poseidon's gift pleased the Earthsider. She never knew such a vessel existed, but then, a great deal had surely changed since when last Olympos and Earth could easily be traversed as one.

Changes leveled by time and distance, it seemed, were not exclusive to Olympos. Amynta snapped at the air to call for the winged steed Lord Poseidon had gifted to her. The steed had the manners of an uneducated man but the heart of a child. If given the proper training Thon would make for a great—

"Ahh, the oiko' of the once and *always* watery Poseidon—did you drain this wittle man of his wife?" The sing-song voice came before its owner fully materialized, but she needed neither to know this particular god. She had made a mistake placing the coins on Deidros. She might as well have called for Mathropos herself.

From the air stepped a bearded man. Before he completely settled on the sands, his angled face shifted to that of an unbearded youth. In his right hand he casually, but deftly, twirled an azure staff topped by a pair of winged snake heads. He wore the garments of a peasant but girdled by a heavy gold chain festooned with all sizes and shapes of coins.

Amynta sighed. "Lord Hermes. I am delighted you've come to bring poor Deidros downward into the Asphodel Meadows. I shall not obstruct your duties." She tried to move past him but the god of trickery and thievery stopped her with his staff.

"Tut-tut-tut, oikonomos. The fisherman has already been ferried to Tartarus for his crimes against the gods. You, on the other hand, you deserve a far more entertaining punishment." He ran the snake heads over her neck, between her breasts, and across her backside.

Amynta grinned. "Lord Hermes, I am flattered by your attentions but my duties for Lord Poseidon take precedence over—"

"Do you miss him?" Hermes circled Amynta, dragging the staff through the sand as he paced around her. The line he created was deep and as the staff moved, so too did the snake heads, biting at the sand. They created black, hairline fractures erupting away from the circle.

"He is my Lord, I am his oikonomos. There is nothing to miss." She knew Hermes had killed Thon, otherwise the stallion would surely have already appeared. Unlike the Fates, Amynta could not as easily engage in a verbal repartee with a god. Nor could she outrun him and she certainly would not be able to best him physically.

"Sweet little Amynta, always the diplomat. It is not your aquatic lord to whom I refer but your deceased husband."

Amynta held her gaze on Hermes. If she could keep him occupied with her grief he might not detect the presence of

Poseidon's treasure against her abdomen. She prepared herself, for Hermes could as easily banish her to Tartarus as he would split her in half with his staff.

Hermes' grin was wide and dark. "Let's palaver, shall we?"

THIRTY-ONE

Laurel slept and dreamed.

She dreamed about myths and of the gods in those stories —lusty and robust, heroic and tragic; so riddled with marital and family problems no Earthsider could ever quite understand.

Abruptly she was nowhere in particular and then she drifted over the Labyrinth. The thick slab walls formed a pattern she recognized but could not remember. To her right there was movement and where she expected to see Daedulus leading Icarus to safety, instead she found Trutina pursuing Poseidon. *But the symbol* she scolded her dream-self, *where have I seen it before?*

The dream blurred and then she found herself hovering over Odysseus' ship—she knew this with that ubiquitous dream knowledge that sometimes accompanies such things. She watched helplessly as it was tossed by Poseidon's wrath, and then inexplicably she was sneaking into Medusa's lair as the gorgon lay in wait for Perseus. Laurel dreamed on, wandering through halls filled with the stories of Herakles conquests, then appeared instantly atop a dais in the center of the Parthenon surrounded by all twelve Olympians. They stood stoic and silent as statues but she knew they were alive. Watching. Judging. Deciding which course her Fate should take. Darkness swept through the image and Mathropos' cackling laugh followed, pulling all color away and splashing it over the columns like blood. Then she was alone with a black haired boy in a dirty chiton who did nothing but cry and would not answer Laurel's questions.

Those dreams gave way to a half-awake state where she stared at the cabin ceiling for long periods of time, not sure if she was still dreaming. She felt the ship gently rocking her, rolled to her left and fully let sleep take her again.

For a while, she mostly drifted. She thought about her life. Indeed, the sage tea had repaired some part of her she didn't know existed. The state of threads from before meeting Paul and after Paul's death, she supposed, were reknitting as one complete tapestry. She did not have the answers she wanted—how and why had Paul kept all of Olympos hidden from her for a year—but she knew her threads had been mended. She knew, too, that Poseidon was alive somewhere and in torment. And yet, he continued reaching out to help her despite the cost.

She pictured him before her and saw that he did not look much different as Poseidon than he did as Paul. He wore his wavy black hair caught up in a ponytail and retained the pelt of salted black hairs gathered at his chest. She watched herself lay on his stomach and lightly stroke his sternum, running her fingers through those hairs, up his neck and into the neatly trimmed night-black Vandyke speckled with white and gray. She heard his voice telling her how much he loved her, how everything had changed, how he would miss her.

The moment began to glow and she settled into it, relishing it.

Without warning, the dream turned on her. Poseidon swelled up and away from her, his body morphing into a grotesque merman, his eyes bulging into those of a fish but his face remained human. She tried to get away from him but his scaly-black tail caught her, crushed her close. She screamed but could only make painful squeaks until finally Poseidon's slimy fingers wrapped around her mouth and silenced her completely.

He carried her through murky currents in a familiar sea, holding her so tight she could barely breathe. They emerged from oily silt into a ship's cabin she knew painfully well. Below them sat her father.

Alone.

Fear and confusion distorted her father's face face as he frantically searched for something. Outside she could hear the metallic cries of the gulls.

Laurel fought the monster-Poseidon in vain, her father falling apart beneath her. The pieces of him became parts of the cabin in the way barnacles attached themselves to pilings of a pier. She wanted to cry, the merman's oils sluiced into her pores and stopped all but her breath and heart. Her chest burned and burned but there was no fire, only the fishy ooze of this Poseidon creature. Below, she watched her father continue to fall apart, piece by piece, never finding what he was looking for and crying out for her.

Laurel! Laurel! Lil'fin! Lil'fin! Laurie! Laurie! His voice changed to Paul's and back to his own, repeating her name like a curse or a punishment.

And then a breeze came upon her and dragged out the heat in her breast, breaking it loose. The merman, the cabin and her father eroded back into flat black nothingness.

Laurel awoke in a sweat, the sheets wrapped tightly around her neck and body.

The owl's head pendant lay beside her on the bed, somehow.

She snatched it up and returned it to where Paul had placed it.

Remember the dream, he'd told her. But what part of the dream? The differences between her myths and the realities of Olympos? The boy? Are you really a monster? Can Trutina be trusted? The last she whispered aloud: "What about my father?"

The vague glow of the orb cast sinuous shadows around the cabin and she would not have been surprised if Mathropos stepped out of the corner. Nothing came at her, though. The only movement: a gentle pitch and sway of the ship riding Olympian waters.

"I'm scared," she said out loud, hoping her words carried to Paul or her father because they seemed to be the only safety and wisdom she could trust. Poseidon? Who knew. Trutina? Something about the Labyrinth in her dream told her to be wary. Icarus? He was too young, too eager, and so loyal that he might well bring down the sky only meaning to carry her to the stars.

She decided to bathe away the dregs of the dream and head topside. There would be no chance of sleep now.

THIRTY-TWO

"There she be, Earthsider. Athena's island nary a cleat's throw off the port bow." the Angler spoke more gently now, his words less halting. He seemed rejuvenated by his rekindled connection to the *Balance*. His slim lips no longer cracked, his gait more agile, if possible; though there still seemed to be a pain in the whites of his eyes. Nonetheless, it was evident that the both of them had received healing. Though the dregs of the dream yet haunted her, Laurel felt close to being done with something vital.

Icarus grinned widely, his boyish charm unshaken. He tightrope-walked along the portside rail toward her; leaping down with perfect form and balance.

Watching the two of them now, Laurel would be the first to deny last night had ever happened. But they all knew, whether catalyzed by the Fates or compounded by her Earthsider presence, they'd come through something together and no amount of manipulation by the Fates could ever unweave that bond.

Laurel scanned the horizon, the early afternoon sky as

handsome and vast as it was before the storms. In the endless blue she saw shadows of the dream and closed her eyes.

"M'lady?" Icarus to her left, his wings fluttering restlessly.

"I'm okay, Icarus. Bad dreams." She opened her eyes, keeping at least one hand hovering over the pendant. Until she reached the second lighthouse she would not truly be mended. But that wasn't entirely true either. She needed Paul to be fully healed.

The horizon remained unbroken for a moment and then a rocky jut of land cut the plane of her view. She looked out over the shimmering azure waters and the land, into the misleading serenity of the blue sky knowing that the Fates waited, carefully assessing her Threads. Each of them trying to find another frayed section to pull apart and reweave.

Thick waves lifted *The Balance* effortlessly where she rested at anchor before they rolled onward to the distant shore. She watched the rocky beach line, as unaware and immortal as the gods themselves, and tried to picture Athena. She thought of what she'd say or how she'd approach the goddess of war. There was no precedent, and Paul had not been honest enough to provide her any protocol for greeting his niece—that was, of course, if some echo of Earthsider myths applied here. Laurel stopped her thoughts and reached for the owl at her neck.

I don't know why you kept all this secret from me.... A whisper of a whisper responded along the path which connected her through the pendant to Paul. But it was not strong enough to be an answer. Laurel knew Poseidon was not free to do as he pleased. She knew he was held somehow, trapped by Mathropos. She had been granted glimpses of his torment, and could only imagine the truth of what he might be suffering. Perhaps this was what he intended for her all along: To journey here and find some truth from Athena.

"Where are the others?" she asked abruptly.

"It's just us, m'lady—we didn't have time to send out the rest of the invitations." Icarus waltzed up beside her.

Laurel let go the pendant, her gaze remained on the island.   "Hera, Hephaestus, Hades, Hermes, Apollo, Artemis, Aphrodite, Ares, Dionysius? The rest of the gods and goddesses. Aren't they supposed to be in this together against the Fates?"

"Ah, well that—" Icarus stopped and stifled the smirk curling his lips. "It is a difficult answer to give easily, m'lady." He produced an apple from a back pocket and bit into it.

Trutina spoke as he came down from the pilot house, "Olympos is dying. The gods disagree as how to best handle the burial arrangements. That is, how do you call it boy? That is the *stretch of it*." The old man's gaze never left the shoreline.

"You don't know that any more than Da. Olympos is *not* dying. It has taken ill, that I'll grant you. Olympos cannot perish so long as she—" Icarus stopped. He studied the apple purposefully, bit into it again.

Trutina cocked his head but did not interrupt.

Laurel turned to face the boy.

Icarus struggled to maintain eye contact.

"What about 'she', Icarus? Is there something you've not told me?"

"You are the lynch pin, m'lady." He blurted and silenced himself again with another chomp on the apple.

Trutina *hrrumphed* and tended to the rigging.

"Am I? What does that mean, exactly?"

The boy took a moment to respond then held up the half-eaten apple by way of example.   "This is sort of what

Olympos is right now." Icarus fumbled through the pockets of his vest until he found an orange. Using the dagger from his belt, he sliced the orange in half and mashed the two fruits together with a juicy squish. "It is my belief that you are here by more than chance alone. I think you can help heal the rift between Earthside and Olympos. But I am singular in this belief." He kept his eyes locked on hers now.

She waited, fully expecting him to break out a joke or a stutter or something but he held himself stoically. Laurel moved closer to him. "I want to know everything," she spoke evenly but did not feel in balance at all.

"Let us finish this elsewhen, boy. We are upon the Isle of Athena and the Earthsider must be properly ferried —"

"I will fly her. One more time, if you don't mind m'lady?" The boy finished the apple and orange fastidiously, tossing the rind and core overboard.

"Icarus. I want to know the stretch of it. Please." Laurel took his hand in hers.

The boy squeezed her hand. "Soon," he said. "I cannot break my oath, m'lady."

Laurel looked into his eyes, their normally depthless brown had hardened.

"We do not have time for theatrics," Trutina observed. "We must begin the proper—"

"It will be me honor to fly you, m'lady." Icarus pulled back from her and bowed.

Laurel wanted to push closer to the truth, but she felt the pull of Athena's island, the pull of a more elusive truth. She said, "I'd be honored to fly with you one last time, Icarus. If you're up to it."

"Hedgeroom, m'lady. We are close enough for this jaunt, trust me." He flexed his wings to their full dimensions, showing handsomely feathered extensions of the boy's ragged mop of hair. The wings fluttered eagerly, poised in preparation for their flight.

"I cannot allow it, boy." Trutina's voice came directly, almost harshly.

Laurel tugged at the pendant.

"I can take the heat, Angler—the seaweed master isn't going to begrudge you half a kilometer for your—"

"Th'distance is irrelevant, Icarus. You know better. This be not a matter of simply completing the task. There is an order of things I am bound to follow by the debt I owe. Stay your wings. Please."

"My apologies, Angler. I meant no disrespect." The boy did not look hurt, nor did he attempt to make a joke. If anything, he seemed to be admiring the old man.

"You know, Earthsider, we don't have much ritual to stand on anymore. Debts are settled with fists and bloodshed more often than with heroism and honor. I think perhaps it is you who will be healing us." Laurel wanted to hug the man but decided that would be pushing it. Instead she made a slight bow at the waist. Then, to fill the awkward silence she asked, "Will we be docking somewhere further up the island? I would be honored to walk with you—"

"No. The docks be far to the east; your place is at the second lighthouse not but three hours walk north along this coast. I shall ferry you as close as can be done among these shoals."

Laurel eyed the coastline, admiring the subtle balance between fine white sand and bold black rock skirting the shore. Further in, the foliage thickened to a wall peppered by fat orange and angry pink blossoms camouflaging any means of accessing the inner reaches of Athena's island.

"And will you do me the honor of escorting me to the—"

"This be not my journey to make, Earthsider."

"Wait? What do you mean? Icky, what does he mean?"

"He and the *Balance* are...that is, when we leave—you and me without him—in other words—"

"I am bound here, Laurel Nash. Such are the consequences of my indiscretions and the bonds of a blood debt. Until this war sees an end and I am reunited with Isoropia, my feet can never leave this deck."

The silence between them held, punctuated occasionally by slaps of waves upon the hull of the *Balance*.

"I didn't know; I guess I always assumed you would be with us."

"It will be my final honor to perform *Hárika ya tin gnorimía* ...the Song of Greeting...to ensure the necessary introductions are made proper; as are the wishes of Athena. Though I and you shall no longer share this deck, know that were I and you to have this dance again, debt or no, I would ferry you 'cross all seas of Olympos to Earthside and back." He pressed her hand into his and whispered: *Tà pánta rheî kaì oudèn ménei.*"

The old man held Laurel's hand a moment and then abruptly broke the embrace, moving away toward the prow.

"Everything flows; nothing stands still," Icarus spoke the translation only after Trutina had reached the prow of the ship where he now stood humming, swaying, conducting the *Balance* closer to Athena's island with minute ministrations; a surgeon suturing capillaries could not be more delicate.

"Icaru...Icky, will he be...what happens after he pays this debt?"

The boy kept his eyes on Trutina. "Your question has two answers. The debt will be paid and he will be Removed."

Laurel turned to look him in the eyes. When she saw the truth there she bowed her head. "I was afraid you would say that. I do not like this place with its customs, rules of the gods, and strange blood debts."

"Atonement of a blood debt carries the highest honor among the gods."

"Debts among men or *gods* never end honorably, Icky."

They watched Trutina for a time as he conducted the ship closer to Athena's shore. His voice, withered but warm, filled the air in lilting harmonies that sounded neither English nor Greek but a pleasant blend of the two.

"Can blood debts be shared or transferred to another, Icarus?"

"Yes. But at great cost to both—oh m'lady no. You cannot bear this burden! M'lady no, please do not interfere you will only—m'lady! Laurel!"

THIRTY-THREE

Icarus released his wings and launched himself into a low hover, prepared to swoop in and snatch the Earthsider from the decks and then carry her to Athena's island, but realized doing so would shift the blood debt to himself. *Curse the bloody blood debt rules!*

He dropped to the deck and ran, using his wings to propel him up and over rigging and railing alike. He was surprised at Laurel's speed and agility but she would not reach Trutina or else Da, Posi, even Hades himself would have his hide and soul as trophies.

"M'lady, please stop—you cannot take this from him! This is a *blood* debt, sealed by sacrifice of life by debtor and payee." Icarus grabbed at her arm, pulling her to a stop.

"Leave me alone, Icarus. To hell with debts and payment —I owe him this. He saved my life *twice* that's payment enough."

"But you are *not* the payment for this debt, Laurel!" She fought him but he subdued her with his wings. Not an easy task for she landed a frenzy of kicks on his shins and toes.

"Remember what he said to you: Everything flows, nothing stands still—this is the way of it, m'lady."

"Let me go, Icarus. He *doesn't* deserve to be Removed."

"Laurel, this is not a wager you can win; you do not want to take this debt from him!"

"I do not care! He doesn't deserve to die, he doesn't have to go this way...he...can't die this way...."

"M'lady, please...listen to me. The gods did not bring this upon him. Trutina chose the payment for himself."

She stopped, going limp against him. Icarus let out a strained sigh of relief. He felt her sobbing against him but did not know what else to say or do. He found himself deeply moved by her love of this man whom she'd only known a few days. "Trutina is indeed a great man; Olympos surely will suffer in his absence. But if the brother gods succeed in this war, he will be restored, touted a hero among the divinity."

He wiped her tears and she wrapped her arms around him tightly. But she did not look at the Angler again. Icarus had only ever witnessed the *Hárika ya tin gnorimía* once before, when he was much younger. The song reminded him of the sound moon beams must make far out on sea with no ears to catch them.

The Balance moved gracefully close among the reefs and breakers peppering Athena's island. Not even Charon could maneuver a craft with such elegance. "I wish I could fly as well as he pilots his ship."

"Am I to be the one who finishes this war?" Laurel whispered, her back to Trutina's song.

Icarus started to answer with a pithy anecdote but silenced himself, for the moment had to remain rhetorical. Near the final chorus he finally did speak to her saying, "I would that I could hoist you up and away directly to Anaktoro, m'lady. To the Underworld with all these goddies and their war, debts, and wicked wicked Fates. If I could, I would fly you directly to Paul."

Laurel laid her hand against his face and smiled warmly. "We will fly again, right? You're coming with me?"

Icarus returned her warmth, knelt down on one knee and gave Oath: "I am your servant to the end, m'lady. May your winds always find comfort in my wings."

"Open with song, close with anchor," Trutina sang at last in English. He squatted to the deck, stroking her timbers lovingly his hands seemed to meld with the wood. *The Balance* understood and released her anchor, ceased her movements and awaited her captain's next command.

"I have only heard about this from Da. He has only seen it twice." Icarus could not stop watching. "You must see this, m'lady."

She did turn, finally, just as Trutina's hands took on the texture of the decking. His neck muscles tightened, his face yellowed but his voice burst forth in a marvelous cacophony of—

"It's a whale song..." Laurel breathed out the words so low Icarus almost didn't hear her.

"Hail? I do not see the similarity between the sound of ice striking the ground and—"

"Whale song.... It's beautiful and frightening...is he... being Removed now?"

"No, he speaks the language of the oceans...it is the final verse of *Hárika ya tin gnorimía*. He tells Athena that Poseidon bade him—Trutina—come for his—Poseidon's—beloved. Just as Trutina has come too to reclaim his beloved."

Thunder bombarded *The Balance* and lightning *krrrackaowwed* back and forth across the sky in a wicked yellow-white scar; the elegant harmonies shook the timbers of *The Balance* knocking Laurel to her knees and Icarus against the portside rail.

"That escalated quickly," Laurel said with a laugh.

"Stay close, m'lady...that did not come from Athena." Icarus knew from whom the stormy display originated. He had seen it before. He had felt it before. He flexed his wings in preparation. *I have been waiting for you*, he thought, pushing it out across his threads.

"*Cease your song, Angler!*" Makaisi's voice resonated from among the clouds, shaking the ship nearly as deeply as her thunder.

"No..." Laurel immediately began shaking as she peeled herself from the deck. Icarus knelt beside her.

"I will protect you, m'lady—I will not allow them to tamper with your threads again." He had to get her off the ship but Trutina had not yet finished the song. "Hurry Angler!" he cried out as he guided her forward to the pilot house.

"They are here *because of me*." She tried to pull away from him but Icarus caught her in his left wing.

Brilliant magnesium-white light wiped the sky of detail, followed by a series of bone-jarring jolts to the hull sending up columns of ocean water in all directions. Icarus held Laurel close until the onslaught ceased.

Plumes of smoke and tongues of fire illuminated the front of *The Balance* where Trutina once stood. Icuars hurried them forward only to find a raw scorched maw in place of the Angler.

"Trutina!" Laurel called and saw immediately that the he had escaped calamity but did not appear to be entirely whole. As he drew himself up, Laurel could see an awful black rip, embedded with wood shrapnel, along the left side of his torso and head.

"Daughter of Nash you have woven your damage and spread your taint *upon this land! Your filthy threads must be sheared, your presence* Removed!"

"Stay here. Help Trutina." Icarus pushed Laurel toward the injured Angler, dropped into a blade-stance and cried out above the noise of Makaisi's storm: "You will not Remove her, witch. Not this time. Not ever." In his head, however, he only heard the screams of his mother—the same sound he heard whenever he was near any of the Fates. He shed his vest and backpack and leapt upward into the maelstrom.

THIRTY-FOUR

Laurel tried to stop the boy but tripped on the menagerie of items lost from his discarded gear. "Icky STOP! Icarus please!" Her voice could not reach him now as he headed into the heavens to confront Makaisi.

"You must depart, Earthsider," Trutina's ruined face could barely form the words. Blood soaked his hair, running down the old scar, turning it black.

"I can't! Icarus! The-the-the song...shit...shit..." *get a hold of yer bones and brains girl,* her father's voice ordered. She did so and tore strips from her chiton and tended to the Angler's wounds

Trutina slapped at her feebly. "Go! The song is complete...the debt paid—you *must* leave this ship before the sister-Fate brings your death."

She ignored him.

"*Come at me boy, I shall reunite you with your pathetic mother!*" Makaisi's voice screeched in crackling glee from somewhere overhead. Icarus was nowhere to be seen.

Angry black-gray clouds had punched their way into existence over Athena's island now, the shoreline shuddered by relentless waves which tossed *The Balance* about as if it were a toy. Laurel caught a glimpse of the Makaisi as she danced within eldritch energies coruscating in and out of the clouds, a few tendrils tickling the mizzen.

"You will not stop the boy. Nor can you ever hope to stop her," Trutina rasped; blood and spit dangled from his mouth.

Laurel doctored Trutina's wounds but could not find the source of his bleeding. His body seemed to be embossed upon the deck rather than separate from it. "Are you leaving me? Is this your Removal?" He did not answer, his eyes rolled in his head.

Pain seized the back of Laurel's head as Makaisi dug her fingers into her scalp, whirling her away from Trutina. The Fate pushed her face against the deck and dragged her along the boards until she crushed her against the base of the pilot house.

A self-satisfied smear of a grin painted her face but Laurel was waiting. "Fear is a wonderful silencer, isn't it Earthsider?"

The opportunity to strike came. Laurel brought her knee up into Makaisi's midsection, catching herself as the Fate released her. She rolled out and up to her knees bringing both fists down upon the woman's back in a hammering blow.

But Makaisi moved faster, catching Laurel's hands and pulling her viciously down into the pilothouse wall. The collision shook Laurel's skull. She had no sense of up, down, right or left but she managed to stagger to the mural, collapsing upon it in a heap.

Makaisi did not hesitate to strike again, this time launching a spear of light directly at Laurel's head.

"M'lady move!" Icarus appeared starboard in a flurry of

wings and rain catching Makaisi at the waist and disappearing up into the skies again.

Laurel did not move soon enough and the blade of light caught the right side of her head, almost directly in the eye. Searing pain passed through her skull like a hot garrote.

"Earthsider!" Trutina had managed to crawl along the deck, his skin a mottled array of wood grain, blood, and rain.

Blood began to fill Laurel's right eye, her vision waffling and her head still ringing with pain. She stood anyway, dizziness churning her stomach. She searched the darkness for some sign of Icarus. Frantically, she pulled another strip from her chiton, pressing it to her eye. "Icarus!" she cried out, rain, thunder, and lighting responded in earnest. But no sign of the boy or the sister of Fate.

"Earthsider, you can delay no longer. You must depart *The Balance*!" Trutina growled as he drew himself up from the deck into a standing position. All color left in his face, seeped out of him into the deckwood.

"I will not leave you and I sure as hell am not going to leave Icarus!" She scanned the deck for a weapon, for something to throw. Trutina grabbed her arms and, impossibly, dragged her to the prow of the ship.

"What the hell are you doing, Trutina?" she could not pry his fingers from her arm.

"Finishing what was begun. I and you are squared, Earthsider—this is the way of it. The boy does as he does of his own accord and you—"

"Stop! You will not throw me from this ship." She pleaded with him. Trutina paused looking into her with his pupiless eyes. "Let me help him. He's just a boy."

Wind lashed *The Balance* and lightning cracked the sky.

She saw Trutina as he once was, full of vigor and life and less a part of the ship, knowing that the war and time and loss had corrupted his existence, turned him into just another plank among many weathered planks in the deck. "Would you not do the same for *Isa*?"

Trutina released Laurel.

She could hardly maintain her balance, the pain in her eye immense, the ringing in her head deafening but she dashed across the deck looking for a boat hook, harpoon, even the lid to a barrel would suffice.

Makaisi screamed overhead and Laurel watched as the Fate spun backward out of a cloud: naked, or at least she was not covered in clothing, her breasts and pelvis wrapped in undulating black smoke while around her arms writhed deadly yellow-white lightning. She lighted upon the aft rail as Icarus glided into view his back to Laurel. One of his wings looked damaged but he seemed otherwise unharmed.

Laurel hefted an awl pike from beneath piles of rope. The rusted tip would look lovely buried in Makaisi's skull. She tried running, stumbled and settled for a swift trot; hell-bent on anchoring the Fate to the railing where she stood.

But Icarus moved with blinding swiftness, swooping down pounding the air with his wings like a human humming bird. He caught Makaisi beneath the arms and hoisted her upward into the clouds, their faces centimeters apart, the woman's arms pinned to her sides.

"Release me you filthy little bird or I will send your skin back to your father in a satchel!"

"We finish this dance, now, *witch!"* Icarus roared back and they disappeared into the darkness.

Light and thunder dotted the clouds and then briefly a few tendrils of lightning silently arced across all of the horizon like the hands of an impossibly large giant.

And then nothing.

No sound.

No lightning.

No thunder.

Laurel could not even hear her own cries, though she could feel her body shaking. She moved but did not move; *The Balance* rocked strongly and stopped, the ocean going sharply and eerily calm.

Trutina approached her but said nothing, watching the empty, dark skies with her.

Silence dropped around them like a bomb, the nothing-ness erupting around the ship.

Then, a single massive blast of thunder shook the sky across the whole of Olympos, splitting it open beyond the blue and black of sky and space.

"Oh," Laurel managed as a thousand arcs of yellow-white lightning skewered the night sky with jagged illumination.

First Makaisi's body fell, then Icarus, hurtling downward in an awful gangly spin of arms and wings.

Bands of moonlight lingered among the waves where turmoil and storm had just rumbled.

"The boy destroyed...a *Fate*." Trutina dropped to the deck before Laurel could catch him. They both watched helplessly as the bodies plummeted downward.

"Icarus!" she cried out, hot pain speared her skull where Makaisi's attack had burned a fat line across her temple and back into her hairline.

The boy did not respond. He did not seem to be conscious and by the time Laurel realized he would crash into the deck of the *Balance* it was too late to do anything.

The boy's body slammed so hard into the wood that *The Balance* shook as if a meteor punctured her deck.

Laurel screamed as she broke into a staggered run, reaching the feather-strewn scar in the center of the mural well before Trutina, who came shouting after her.

THIRTY-FIVE

"Please don't be dead, please...oh please...please? Trutina? Trutina! Help me get to him!"

Laurel waited impatiently for the ruined Angler, her words came between shudders that traveled the length of her body. Her skull throbbed, blurring her vision, her thoughts as tumultuous as the recent storm. The vision in her right eye had returned but the flesh above and along her temple was seared, raw to the touch. She turned and started to lower herself into the hole Icarus' fall had made while Trutina countered her weight with his own.

"You can delay your departure no longer, Earthsider. Alive or dead, the boy can aid you no longer."

"It doesn't matter. Your stupid war, your stupid gods—he did this because of me."

"Aye. As have we all done what must be done because of you."

Laurel stopped her descent and took in the damage Trutina had suffered. Several thick slivers of wood lodged in his scalp and along the side of his neck. The man's body had been cooked, the skin of his torso rippled and reddened, blackened and torn by flame and wood.

"I..."

"There are worse debts to owe," he said and she knew instinctively that the man had given up his Removal for her.

"See to him," he continued, the words came in shards from his quivering mouth. "But if you tarry any longer then even I cannot bear such a debt."

Laurel nodded and left the Angler at the edge of the hole and made her way down to the boy.

Liquid streams of silver moonlight fell around and into the hole, illuminating the blood slick feather-coated heap below her. His body remained motionless, partially covered by deckwood and plaster, pots and pans strewn amongst the rubble. His head lay left side up, facing the entrance to the galley and for a swift moment Laurel thought she saw him blink. But as she neared him, her eyes lighted upon his twisted limbs and bloody feathers—finally halting on the severed right wing laying crosswise over his back.

At the bottom, Laurel retrieved a glow-orb from the debris. "Oh...Icky...."

The boy did not move and his voice crackled hardly more than a dry leaf rasping at a screen door. *"oh...m'lady, what bringss you...here?"*

Laurel broke into heaving sobs, fighting hard to quell them; she leaned forward then decided to just lay fully down beside the boy, looking directly into his face.

"Hello. Have I been alsee...." His eyes rolled in his head showing bloody whites.

Laurel put her hand on his face and he smiled.

"I fell again...."

"No no no....shhh...you...." but she could not say he was

going to be alright. His body lay in a question mark, the severed wing had already lost its luminence; the remaining left wing twitched and fluttered involuntarily.

"Mmm'lady...do not cry...it makes you saahhhhh...." His voice caught and his body quivered in violent bursts.

"Icky...tell me what to do? I need to—"

"Smile for me, m'lady...show me thosssss peely.... Pearly. Pearly.   Perrrrrrrrrrrlies...." With every broken word or missing letter Icky's body twitched, his eyes could not find their place.

"You stopped her. You saved us."

He smiled a mix of blood and teeth.

"You...go...." He managed clearly if not more gravelly. *"I will dance with you again mum...."* With that he stopped moving abruptly, his eyes slowly stuttering closed, his wing quiet.

Laurel did not leave immediately, lying beside her hero a while longer, damn the sisters and debts. She did not sleep and only moved at the last when she no longer felt the weight of her body. She stood easily, taking up a loose feather. Avoiding the debris, Laurel made her way through the galley and to her room.   Quietly and surprisingly steady, she undressed and donned a pair of khaki slacks and a plain blue Henley tee. She reached beneath her pillow and slid Dad's journal out and into her back pocket. Then, methodically, Laurel pulled her hair back in a wad, doused her face with water and stood staring at nothing.

Laurel returned to the grave. She paused only to kiss Icarus on the forehead before climbing out and onto the deck of *The Balance*. She hugged Trutina who said: "I shall ferry him home, Earthsider. To his Da."

Laurel nodded, but said nothing. She took hold of the

pendant. It was cold and empty but she was not surprised. She slipped Icarus' feather into her hair and left *The Balance* for Athena's island.

THIRTY-SIX

Mathropos felt Makaisi's death in the same way a fly might feel the hand of she who crushed the life from it. Had she not held so many threads the death surely would have shaken her more. Surely.

But she knew before the moment arrived that Makaisi's threads were nearing the end of their use. She'd laid the majority of that pattern herself, so why be shocked or give way to any iota of remorse? And yet she felt like weeping, felt hot vengeance rising in her gut. Both of which she stifled with a thought, though a slight tremor rippled through her hands.

The moist air of Poseidon's trabeated mausoleum clung to the undersides of her breasts and slickened her back in a most distasteful manner. Still, she admired the simple straight trajectory of the lintels crossing overhead. Like threads, they traveled true from one point to another—not at all like her current circumstances, which had now become like that of the accursed sands of a beach: *always shifting, always changing*.

Makaisi had failed, though her death certainly would be

a gift to unwrap later. But without the Judge to collect the Earthsider, Mathropos would have to maintain the well-being of the god of the oceans long enough to lure the Earthsider to Anaktoro.

A risk, she knew. Trusting Mira with the task would be like asking a child to wrestle Minos' bull. Something would have to be done about the fat one but not until other threads had been tied off. And then there remained the matter of the *Dunamis*, lost or stolen or hidden somehow by the wretch currently suspended between lintels above her. If only she could peel his threads from his desiccated form one by one, savoring each millimeter of his life as he watched...Oh sweet elation would fill her then.

As if on cue the trident-wielder shuddered, and a noise like that of a seed pod being crushed escaped his parched lips.

She did not need to check the security of his shackles but drifted up to him just the same. Reaching out to the thick cords from which Poseidon dangled, her right hand seized in mid-air, spasmed futilely, and went limp briefly before she regained control. In the fleeting moment of rebellion, Mathropos witnessed eleven snippets of the lives of those whose threads she had recently consumed.

Poseidon remained immobile, unconscious. He could be nothing more for he hung from his own threads, a torture not even a god could endure for long. She wanted to take just one, savor the earthy and robust richness only a god's threads could provide—the skin covering her face lurched forward and a thousand frayed threads screeched outward.

Mathropos dropped to the tiled floor surrounding the pool with such force cracks spider-webbed out from her compressed and shuddering form. "This will not do," her voice shrilled. "This will not do." She spoke again, pressing down her skin, tucking back threads, and rising from the floor with all the grace she could muster.

She scanned the room unnecessarily for no one would dare disturb her here other than Makaisi or Mira. One was dead and the other...Mathropos looked up into Poseidon's open eyes glaring down at her.

"Her arrival brings your death too." Blood coated his once shell-white teeth, his face had taken on the texture and pallor of a seahorse but his voice remained resonant, commanding.

Mathropos grinned back at him, making a considerable effort to hide the turmoil raging beneath her skin. "Words, Lord Poseidon, do not hold sway over Fate."

"Aye. But then when has Fate ever been swayed by anything less?" he chuckled and then slowly submerged into an unconscious stupor.

Fly up, rip him from the lintels, choke him with his own Threads while you suck them from—

"Sister! Makaisi has fallen!"Mira burst in, wailing, blubbering, and threw herself against the wall in typical melodramatic overindulgence.

"Stop it, you oaf. I am already aware of her failure." Mathropos did not look up at the dying god—*you mean you cannot, you weakling*—her hands taut to her sides, lips fixed in a sneer she fought for control and won. "Get up. We have to prepare for our guest."

Mira peeled herself from the floor, her eyes lingering on the depression in the tile. "We should not proceed any further until father returns." Her tone defiant, the youngest sister of the Fates did not have the backbone to back it up, however.

"Always nattering, always meandering! You have no

stomach for this game, Mira. You are too short sighted to realize how marvelous the *Theosophane* has become!"

"You promised the war would bring father back fr—"

Mathropos struck Mira so hard blood spilled from her nose, freckling the wall behind her in red.

"Silence. I can see far along the Threads, sister. Farther than you or Makaisi ever could—once we have the Earthsider and the *Dunamis* we shall control the Bridge and return Olympos to its former glory. And it shall be you and I who rule over the gods *and* Earthsiders!"

Mira's face had hardened. But she nodded consent.

"You bring these moments upon yourself, dear sister. Fret not over the loss of Makaisi, her passing grants us her both a portion of her gifts." *And soon your passing will grant me all the powers of Fate to wield.* Mathropos gently stroked Mira's hair and remembered when they were little girls. They often sat and braided each other's hair, telling stories about the lives of those who's Threads they'd spun and cut that day. "Sister, will you retrieve Makaisi's robes so that we may put her to rest properly?"

Mira said nothing for a long while. Her eyes were closed, her breathing subdued. *Just like when we were girls and father told us the story about the Moiragetes, the Earthsiders: Those who are bound to Olympos...bound to us.* "This will heal Olympos, *Clotho.*" Mathropos smiled despite the undulating pain beneath her skin that seemed to spear into her very bones. She had not spoken her sister's pet name since long before the war.

"Will it be this way after, Mathr—" A quick smile and then just as quickly: "Atropos? It has been so long since we were girls. Sister, can you see that far ahead?" Mira practically cooed.

Mathropos smiled broadly, the apex at both sides of her

grin cracked and split, revealing black threads eager to be released. Fortunately, Mira remained facing away from her and could not see the momentary loss of control. *I see your death and my rise. I see the gods bowing before me as once they made us submit. I see the Earthsiders cowering as I consume their pathetic threads—*

Then she saw what she had to do and it was marvelous. Father had always told her if you love the Weave it will love you back. And the Weave had seen fit to give her every pawn she needed all at the same time in the same place. She stroked Mira absently, tiny black whips lashed out from the pink tissue around her eyes trying to snag a piece of Mira's hair. "Oh, little sister...I see a shade of wonderful things to come. Wonderful things, indeed."

ABOUT THE AUTHOR

I thrive on creative chaos.

This (partially) explains why it's taken me over 15 years to write this book. It started on a beach, actually, when my wife and I were standing on the shore, letting the gentle waves kiss our feet. She watched the horizon, and we listened to the gulls and just kept our happy silence a moment.

Then she turned to me and said, "Poseidon is happy...he must be in love."

That spawned an idea I could not let go of and so I wrote about it.

The other thing that kept me from completing this book is simply procrastination. Well, maybe there's a dash of the hustle and bustle of life thrown in there. Raising 8 children to adulthood. A full time teaching career that spanned 15 years. Voice acting and audiobook narrating.

But mostly procrastination.

I have the next two books already completed, thank goodness, and I'm planning the next series in the realm of Ocean Salt. Hopefully it won't take me 15 years to finish it.

Oh, about the author! Yes!

I am a husband, father, and homesteader. I live with my family on a little place George & Lennie would've been proud of in the sunny southern state of Tennessee. This is my first full length novel, but if you're clever, you can find the first two shorter works I published. Hint: they have nothing to do with Greek mythology.

Thank you for reading my story.

Have a blasty-blast day!

9 781736 149324